C000099785

What has two heads, ten eyes and ter

10012020

Fiction   SHORT STORIES

Talbot Heath School

WHAT HAS TWO HEADS, TEN EYES, AND TERRIFYING TABLE MANNERS?

An Anthology of Science Fiction Horror

Edited by
Sawney Hatton

Published by Dark Park Publishing

Cover design by Armin Numanovic

1st Ebook Edition: May 2014
1st Print Edition: July 2014
This Print Edition ISBN: 978-0-9886444-2-7

DARK
PARK
PUBLISHING

For Dan O'Bannon,
John Carpenter,
and Don Coscarelli,
whose works inspired this book.

CONTENTS

Foreword

Sawney Hatton

"In space no one can hear you scream."

That's the memorable tagline for the 1979 Sci-Fi Horror masterpiece **Alien**. The film, one of my earliest introductions to R-rated fare, left an indelible impression on me. I still recall my elementary school classmate showing off the photo-novel during our lunch period. Who could ever forget the gory "chestburster" scene, or H.R. Giger's surreal production design?

I loved it.

For millennia, Mankind has recognized the frightening aspects of scientific exploration. While it's great that we have uncovered the knowledge to explain so many things that once had mystified us (and that we had mostly attributed to the work of gods), such empirical endeavors have invited the ominous question: *what terrors hath we wrought?*

Genetically modified organisms. Super sentient viruses. Mind-controlling technology.

Hideous mutants borne of atomic radiation. Bloodthirsty aliens guided to Earth by our interstellar beacons. Mal-functioning robots bent on destroying their human masters.

Power-hungry scientists plotting to crush the world via their doomsday inventions.

Yeah, progress can be scary stuff.

Authors have long been writing about such portentous themes. From Mary Shelley's mad Dr. Frankenstein bringing new life to a towering figure of stitched-together body parts, to H.G. Wells's fantastical tales of Morlocks, Martians, and Beast Folk, to John W. Campbell, Jr.'s novella *Who Goes There?*—adapted into the chilling motion pictures **The Thing From Another World** (1951) and **The Thing** (1982)—readers throughout history have had a healthy fear of that which is supposed to make their existence better.

Or at least preserve it.

This anthology features more than a dozen previously unpublished short stories by all different authors (plus a bonus classic by Sir Arthur Conan Doyle) combining Horror and Science Fiction elements. Throughout these pages there are many surprises in store for fans of both genres. The original tales range from the horrifying to the humorous, the subtle to the shocking, the thought-provoking to the thought-twisting. I hope readers will be pleased with the contents of this collection, and I encourage them to seek out other works by the authors they enjoy.

While it is satisfying to see how far the human race has come, it is perhaps wise to remember that, though we may no longer live in the Dark Ages, the light sometimes illuminates things that had best remained in the shadows.

~S. Hatton
May 2014

Microwave Technology

Evan Purcell

Dickie's palms covered my eyes. My left eye was no longer swollen, but it was a little sensitive. I didn't tell him that. That would only make him upset.

That would only ruin the surprise.

"Can I look?" I asked.

"Almost there," he said. Dickie's voice was always very deep. I liked when it sounded happy too.

With his guiding presence behind me, I walked another few steps. I could tell from the hard linoleum under my feet that we were now in the kitchen.

"Now?" I asked.

"Now." He pulled his hands away from my face.

At first, I didn't see anything different about the kitchen. The same sink. Same oven. Same clock on the wall. Then I noticed an entire wall—rows of shelves overlaid with floral wallpaper—was gone. In its place, a steel box about the size of our refrigerator. It had a single, circular window in the front, and nothing but darkness inside.

It looked like something from that movie *Forbidden Planet*.

"What is it?" I asked. I made sure that there was more excitement than confusion in my voice. I wanted to sound excited for my husband.

"It's a Radarange microwave oven," he answered. "It's brand new!"

My brain paused for three seconds. "Oh, how wonderful! A Radio-range!"

"Radarange," he corrected me. "It runs on microwave technology."

I didn't know what that meant. "Wonderful!"

"Isn't it?" He waited for me to respond. I got the impression he wanted me to walk over and touch its glass screen, but he was still grasping my shoulders.

"It's so... big," I said. Probably about six feet tall and another three feet wide. Without the window, it would look almost exactly like a metal refrigerator.

"Powerful," he added. "You can use it for leftovers. It's called re-heating."

"I see," I said. "Does it use gas?"

For a second, Dickie's eyes flashed in anger and I didn't know why. "I just said it uses microwaves. No gas. No fire. No heated coals. Please listen to me." He clenched his jaw muscles for a second, just a second, and then he was back to smiling and crinkling the skin around his eyes. But all it took was that moment—that jaw-clenched moment—to realize why he wanted to surprise me with this new machine.

It was a peace offering, a big metal apology for last month. I almost felt my still bruised right eye, but then I jerked my hand away. Surely, Dickie wouldn't want to be reminded of last month. Especially after such an expensive present.

"Are you happy?" Dickie asked me. He still held my shoulders instead of my hand.

"So happy," I answered.

"Truly?"

"So, so happy," I said.

He kissed me on the cheek and I purred.

The very next day, I used the machine for the first time. It was a Tuesday. I reheated meatloaf from Sunday. I was quite good at meatloaf. Dickie always said it was his fifth favorite dish of mine.

The machine worked as it was supposed to. Dickie made sure to read the twelve-page instruction booklet to me so I would understand all the buttons and dials. He skipped over the parts about safety and maintenance, so I re-read the booklet when he was at work.

At the dinner table, Dickie moaned with delight and said, "This is even better than when it was fresh."

"I'm glad you like it, dear."

He frowned. "Why aren't you eating any of yours?"

I looked down at my meal. I hadn't realized that I'd spent the last five minutes sliding my fork through the meat piles, leaving figure-eights of brown gravy across my plate. I hadn't actually taken even one nibble.

"I'm sorry, dear. I…"

"Well?" he said, staring at my fork as it quivered in my hand.

I ate my first bite. The immediate sensation was one of recognition. I recognized the taste, and that was comforting. I knew what my meatloaf should taste like, and this was correct. But as soon as I swallowed, I felt like there was something wrong with the mouthful—like the meat had been cooked from the middle and bits of it had been turned inside out. I wasn't sure what it was, but it was definitely wrong.

"Delicious," I said.

"Have another bite," Dickie urged.

So I did. I had two more bites, and I felt like each one was stuck at the base of my throat, burning and festering.

"Now isn't that delicious?" he said. "You should be proud of yourself."

"Thank you, dear. I couldn't have made it so quickly without…" I'd almost said *the machine*. "Without the microwave."

Two days later, I noticed a hairline crack in the window display.

Dickie sat in the living room, reading the newspaper. Probably about the presidential debates. He loved those.

I looked around the corner, trying to tell if he was in a good mood. Or at least a neutral mood. I wouldn't want to disturb him if he was less than neutral. I saw that the edges of his mouth curved upwards, into the ghost of a smile. It wasn't much, but it was something. I decided to tell him.

"Dickie dear," I said. Pleasantly. Quietly.

"Yes?" He slipped the pipe from his mouth.

"Could you come here?" I asked. "Just for a second." Again, pleasantly, quietly.

"Of course."

With a mighty show of effort, he folded the newspaper, set it on the sofa, raised himself to his feet, and strode toward the kitchen.

God, he was so handsome. Any woman alive would be jealous of me. He had TV star hair, broad shoulders, and a square chin. He looked like a provider. Whenever he decided that he wanted kids, he wouldn't even need to buy new father clothes. He already looked the part.

I didn't realize until he entered the kitchen that I was standing as far away from the microwave as I possibly could.

"What is it, dear?" he asked.

"I just… I love it so much." I probably should have said "microwave" instead of "it," but he knew what I was talking about.

"Of course you do," he said. "There're only two thousand on the market."

"Dickie, I love it. It's great. But…"

"Well, two thousand, five hundred."

"I think there's a crack in the glass. And I'm worried…"

Dickie marched across the kitchen and instantly reached out his fingers toward the crack. He'd spotted it right away—small and slender and spiraled. It looked like a worm, or a snake poised to strike.

"This?" he asked.

His fingertip traced the outline. Twice.

"Yes," I said. "I don't know anything about microwaves, but aren't you worried that something will... escape?"

Dickie sighed. He wiped his brow. And in a sudden jolt of movement, he balled his hand into a fist and punched the glass. One. Two. Six times. After a seventh, his knuckles were bloody and his chest was heaving.

The crack didn't spread.

"I think we're good," he said.

For the next ten or so minutes, I carefully bandaged his knuckles. His blood caked under my fingernails.

"I'm sorry," he said.

"I know."

"You just don't understand what you do to me sometimes," he continued. His voice sounded broken and gravelly.

"I couldn't possibly," I said, and left it at that.

I twisted the telephone cord around my pinky. Dickie always told me not to do that, it would mess with the wires. But Dickie wasn't home.

"I don't know, Patricia," I said. "I'm afraid of it. I'm afraid of what it could do to us. It's a new technology, and it doesn't seem... Who knows what it can...?"

"What? Like creating giant ants?" Patricia asked. Her voice crackled through the phone.

"You know that's not what I mean," I said. "I don't know anything about microwaves. What about... what about when Dickie says it's time to have a child? What if... oh, I don't know."

My sister waited for me to finish the thought, which of course I didn't. Eventually, she said, "I think you're over-reacting."

I sighed. "You're probably right. I'm not in the kitchen every waking hour of the day, after all."

"Even if you were," she said, "there's nothing dangerous about microwaves. Otherwise, why would they sell them all across America?"

"They're not," I admitted. "He said there's only a couple thousand."

"But surely the people in the factory have tested things," she reassured me. "Surely they know what they're doing."

Patricia was probably right. I always felt more at ease after speaking with her. I always felt like I'd been deflated, in a good way.

"How are Frank and the kids?" I asked.

Either she didn't hear my question, or she chose to ignore it.

"No. That's not all that's bothering you," she said. "The microwave. There's something else, too." Anyone else would have phrased that as a question.

And for once, I decided to say what was on my mind. "It's Dickie. He's… he's not like he used to be. Angry all the time. Very short with me. And last night, I tried to tell him about the cracks in the glass, and he went wild. He punched the glass, over and over and over, until his knuckles bled and I had to calm him down. God, Patricia. I don't know…"

She laughed. "Your life is perfect. Sometimes you just need to learn to appreciate that."

"But he—"

"Christ, Margaret! You have no idea how good you have it."

I didn't want to talk anymore. I should've clicked off the phone and switched on the radio. I should've left that room. But I couldn't stop myself. I had to say it.

"He hit me."

I waited.

Patricia didn't answer.

I almost repeated myself, but I couldn't stand to utter those words again. I was about to pretend that I had never said anything at all, but Patricia stopped me.

"I know," she said somberly.

"You know what?"

She paused for five long seconds. I counted. Finally, she said, "I know about his temper. I've always known."

Sunlight streamed through the living room window. A few smudges on the glass became shadows on my face. I made a mental note to wipe them clean.

"You've always known about…"

"Yeah," Patricia said. "Intuition. I'm your sister."

I could hear tiny voices over the phone. Her children playing and shouting.

When I didn't say anything else, she added, "Can I give you some advice?"

"Please."

"You're beautiful," she said. "And you're clean. I've been to your house, and it's immaculate. You do amazing work as a housewife… but sometimes, a husband just wants more. Dickie works very hard, you know."

"I know."

"I guess what I'm saying," she continued, "is maybe you can try a little harder. You know? Then maybe he won't get in those moods as much."

"What should I do?" I asked.

Patricia sighed. I could barely hear her over the screams of her sons and daughter. "I don't know," she said. "I don't know."

I slept well that night. I didn't dream, of course, but I was restful. Dickie only snored a little.

Then, at 2:30 in the morning, I woke up. There were noises. Not like snoring. These were other sounds, coming from the kitchen. Bubbling and gurgling. Sloshing, too. So many different sounds. It made me think of chemicals, of acids eating away at metal objects.

I nudged Dickie gently. "Wake up, Dickie," I said. "Wake up."

He grunted.

"Dickie, please. There's something downstairs."

In his groggy, half-asleep voice, he mumbled, "Burglars. Must be burglars."

I prodded him harder this time. "Please," I said. "Listen. Don't you hear that… sloshing?"

He struggled to sit upright. He creaked his head toward me. "That's it? That's the noise you woke me up for? It's probably a hose leaking in the yard."

"It's not the hose," I said. "And it's coming from inside, downstairs."

"Goddamn burglars," he grumbled, and went back to sleep.

I had no choice, so I headed downstairs alone. My nightdress was thin, and the air was chilly. I got goosebumps up my arms. I was afraid to find out what was making those noises, but I was even more afraid *not* knowing.

Even before I reached the kitchen, I could see the light. The house was dark enough, and the sky moonless, so I noticed it as soon as I stepped off the staircase. Something was glowing unnatural and green, and it was coming from the kitchen.

"Hello?" I whispered.

No answer.

Why did I do that? Now it knew I was coming.

It.

I wasn't sure why my mind immediately thought of *it*. This intruder could be a *he,* or a *them.* But no. Deep down, I knew *it* was an *it.*

When I entered the kitchen, I saw it right away.

There, behind the cracked glass of the microwave, was something. Some thing.

I couldn't look straight at it because my eyes hurt from the glow, but it appeared to be a long, slithering tentacle, radiating neon green. Behind it were sparks of other colors— pink, yellow, orange. All bright. All neon. Bubbles, perhaps? Eyes?

I glimpsed a world on the other side of that microwave, and I was grateful that I couldn't gaze at it directly.

The tentacle tapped on the glass. It sensed me. It wanted me to notice. It wanted me to tap back.

For a second—an awful second—I felt my body inch forward, as if I actually desired to reach out and touch that thing. But I didn't. I couldn't.

I knew it would take me.

I squeezed my eyes shut.

Stop it, I told myself. *Stop it.*

When I reopened my eyes, the glow was still there. Brighter now. And my head throbbed.

I ran into my bedroom and plunged under the covers. I wanted to force myself back to sleep, but I knew that wouldn't work.

I didn't tell Dickie.

The next night, Dickie didn't come home for dinner. I worried about him. He was seldom late, and when he was, it was usually a bad thing. At 9:15, he limped into the living room. His breath told me he'd come from a bar.

"Dickie, are you…?"

"Dinner," he demanded. "Hungry." He followed me into the kitchen.

"Yes," I replied. "Of course. I had pork chops ready, but then you… Maybe we should go out to a restaurant. After such a day, why don't you treat yourself?"

He grunted. "I'm in no shape to drive anywhere."

"Okay. Maybe we could—"

"Why isn't there any food?" he asked.

"There was," I said. "But you never came home, so I put it back in the fridge for—"

"Take it out," he ordered. "Heat it up. It's easy for you to do that now."

He waited for me to act. I shuffled my feet to the fridge. I pulled out the Tupperware container from it. I poured its contents—a grayish slice of pork—onto a plate.

He watched me, wordlessly, anticipating me to open the microwave and place his food inside.

I held the pork plate tightly in my hands. I would've put it in the microwave, I really would've, but fear stopped me.

"There's something inside it!" I blurted.

Dickie smiled. "Something inside the microwave? More food? Well, take it out."

"It's not food."

Dickie's neck vein bulged. His face flushed red. "What are you getting at?" he asked.

I knew I shouldn't have said anything. I knew he didn't deserve my ungratefulness. But my fear was too much, just too much.

"I'm afraid of the microwave," I said. "Afraid of what's inside it. This new technology... it's not natural."

Dickie's whole body seemed to flare up, like he was a balloon. He was not a large man—he stood barely an inch taller than me—but he could make himself seem massive. He didn't blink at all.

"You're pulling this shit again," he yelled.

"Dickie. Language. I was just—"

He stormed through the kitchen and slammed his still-bandaged fist into the glass screen. *Bam*

"There?" he said.

Bam

"Are you happy?"

Bam

"Do you want to keep hurting me like this?"

Bam Bam Bam

His cuts surely starting bleeding again. I began to cry. He yelled some more, but I couldn't make out what he was saying.

I saw the things on the other side of the glass. They were neon green and yellow—a little pink, too—but they weren't shining as brightly as last night.

They shivered.

"Dickie," I said. "Look. Just look."

He squinted into the glass. For a moment, I thought he could see them, too. But then he shook his head and huffed.

"You don't see the shapes?" I asked, incredulous.

He punched the glass once more. Nothing shattered. It didn't spiderweb.

"I don't see nothin'!" he roared.

"Be careful," I said. "Those things will suck you inside. They'll take you, Dickie!"

"You've gone mad," he said, his voice flat. He studied me. He made faces too. But I just looked over his shoulder.

A lone tentacle, thin as wire, thrust through the crack in the glass. It poked forward, poked toward Dickie. It stroked his hair.

He didn't notice.

"I'm not crazy," I said. "They'll get you. They'll pull you in."

Without saying another word, he picked up the plate of cold pork and placed it in my hands.

23

"You want me to… reheat?" I asked.

He regarded me with something like sadness on his face and left the kitchen.

Maybe I was crazy. I didn't know anything about microwaves, but they had to be safe, right? I was a grown woman frightened to be in the same room as a machine.

I can do this, I told myself.

I looked down at the pork. It was not a good cut. It was too fatty.

I can do this. This is what Dickie wants.

I made a choice at that moment. I chose to ignore my irrational fears and listen to Dickie. I opened the microwave and peered inside. It was dark and empty in there. I didn't see any shapes.

Of course I didn't.

I slid the plate into position.

Still nothing. No shapes at all.

How long did the manual suggest I cook a slab of pork? Eight minutes? Ten?

No shapes.

I leaned closer, to be certain. Was that just a reflection of the light behind me?

Another, bigger tentacle extended out of the dark and wrapped around my waist. I felt barbed suction cups piercing my blouse and digging into my skin. I was squeezed and torn and I never felt so much physical pain in my life.

In an instant, I was drawn inside.

And that's why I'm here now, sitting and waiting. I'm sure things will feast on me sometime, but I've given up being afraid of them.

I can see my kitchen from here, but I can't get to it. So I just sit and wait. I used to wonder where Dickie was. Now I scarcely think about him at all.

Oh, and there are shapes. All around me, in this strange world, there are shapes. I've never seen so much neon!

My eyes ache, but at least there are colors.

And in a way, they're much more beautiful than anything out there.

Crooked Head

Steve Billings

The Eastbound tube train clatters into the station, and my heart sinks when I spot the contorted face of Choler pressed up against the carriage window. Odious little bastard. A toothless grin breaks under his ridiculously bulbous nose, but it's wasted on everyone else here.

He raises a gnarled index finger and points silently towards me. I summon the courage to wink back at him as he explodes into a fit of rage, pounding his filthy, scabrous fists against the glass. The effect of this typical pantomime is dulled somewhat by the total absence of sound, like watching a scene from a surreal horror movie with no plot or reason.

Cassie and I jump into the near-empty compartment at the rear of the train. I scan the rest of occupants to see if any more of the usual suspects are lurking here, but it seems safe enough. Just a mid-morning smattering of tourists poring over guidebooks and office workers heading in for a late start.

I pull the small notebook from my coat pocket and add another entry:

27th October. Paddington Station (Circle Line). Choler.

"Chin up," says Cassie, clasping my hand and resting her head on my shoulder.

The smell of her pineapple-scented shampoo is sufficient to prove she is real enough, and for the moment Choler's rabid gesticulations are pushed from my mind by an over-whelming feeling of relief that I'm not fighting this alone.

I slide the notebook back into my pocket, swapping it for the large plastic pill bottle. I shake the last of the vile yellow capsules free. I swallow it with a grimace, to the consternation of the elderly Japanese couple opposite me, who return hastily to studying their map.

The rest of the journey to Euston Square passes without further interruption. As we head towards the relative sanctuary of the street, I turn to see Choler offering me a parting wave. I quickly check around me before giving him a less cordial hand gesture of my own. He balls his fists and smashes them into the seat in a show of unrestrained fury.

Stand your ground, my old man used to say. Never run from your problems. I'm trying but I really don't know how much longer I can keep this up.

As we reach the surface, I scope the faces in the sea of humanity that swashes past us. A gaggle of secretaries plan their Friday night out, while a pinstriped egotist bawls-out some poor unfortunate at the other end of his phone.

Try looking through my eyes, dickhead, and then you'll have something to moan about.

The meeting at Goetia's opulent headquarters follows the same, tiresome agenda.

Seated around the monstrous conference table are myself, Cassie, and my legal rep, Seth Parkes. We are outnumbered four to one by an army of psychiatrists, chemists, lawyers, and senior suits, all representing the global might of Goetia Pharmaceuticals.

"Do they really need so many people?" whispers Cassie under the pre-meeting hubbub.

This farce has been playing out for months. Goetia tries to persuade me that I'm as mad as a hatter, while I try to assure them that I'm certainly not. In the meantime, the lawyers bandy Latin phrases endlessly back and forth and rack up huge legal bills. It's all a sham and they know it.

Why invite me up to London from the very middle of nowhere once every fortnight, fully expensed, if they have nothing to hide? They've got a problem and they'll have to own up one of these days. The reason they've got a problem is that I'm not the only one seeing things.

Goetia's patroniser-in-chief, Fisher, kicks off the proceedings.

"So, Jack, how are things?" he asks, with the least sincere smile I've ever seen.

"Shit," I reply honestly.

Cue mutterings and furtive glances around the table.

"Go on," he says.

"The sightings are happening a lot more often now, and they seem to be getting weirder every time."

As with each previous meeting, I produce my notebook and read out the list of encounters, from the time of my last visit to my run-in with Choler this morning. The physiatrists scribble furiously, their reactions ranging from sage head-nodding to expressions of sheer incredulity. I recall my experiences with some of the more benign characters like OCD, Hookworm, and Old Maid, and those at the more sinister end of the scale: Slammer, Drench, and Cataract.

I also introduce them to two new ones.

The first I've nicknamed The Beggar, who would have passed for just another solitary down-and-out in the subway, except for the soundless rattle as I dropped the coins into his battered polystyrene cup.

The other is a tired-looking young woman who seems lost in a perpetual trance. Her long dark hair spills over a faded death metal T-shirt emblazoned with the name "Kallix" in bold, gothic lettering. So that's her name.

(Goetia's shrinks encouraged me to name the sightings so I can somehow personalise them and therefore reduce the fear. At least that's the idea. I assure them that when you've seen Scowler sitting on your toilet at six in the morning, it makes scant difference what you call him or anybody else.)

I know Fisher's list of questions by heart.

"Have you noticed any change in their behaviour?"

"Not really. Some of them seem lost in their own little worlds, but most of them are just very pissed off."

"Anything else? Can you smell or touch them?"

I shake my head.

"So you just see them, nothing else?"

"No, he just sees them," hisses Cassie, as I nearly drop the scalding contents of my coffee mug onto my lap. "Isn't that enough, or would like him to suffer in all five senses?"

"Of course not," says Fisher. "I wasn't trying to trivialize Jack's delusions."

"Delusions? It's thanks to you lot that he's here in the first place!"

A senior suit attempts to interrupt her. "I don't think this is helping—"

"That's the whole point! Nothing's helping." Cassie's voice starts to quaver. "You're doing nothing to help him."

I reach for her hand, glad for the chance to show her support for a change.

There is an awkward lull.

"Do you mind if I ask one more question before we wrap things up?" asks Fisher.

"Go ahead," I answer.

"What about Crooked Head?"

I feel like he's just stretched across the table and slapped me in the face.

"No," I reply meekly.

"Still just the one sighting so far?"

I nod.

How many times would he like me to see him? I should respond with something suitably sarcastic, but the mention of that name has left me reeling.

We conclude the meeting in the usual fashion, as I exchange my empty tablet bottle for a new one. The pills in this batch are cobalt blue. God only knows what they've tweaked this time. The colour changes with every visit but the taste only seems to get worse.

"Is there anything else?" inquires Fisher, glancing at his watch.

It's 12:52. The meeting is scheduled to finish at one o'clock. It's obvious he's got a more pressing appointment elsewhere, probably a lunch engagement.

"Yes there is," blurts Cassie. "When are you going to do something other than keep switching his pills? He's still off work, and London's a long way to come every fortnight just to collect these stupid tablets."

"I can assure you, Cassie, we're working day and night on this. The professional opinion of the committee at the moment is that he is suffering from paranoid delusions brought about by conditions unknown."

"That's bullshit," barks Cassie. "What about Randall Holt?"

Don't go there, Cassie, I think to myself.

Fisher casts a glance to his gang of lawyers. A simple shake of their heads tells him all he needs.

"You know we can't discuss other claimants. You should also be aware that Jack has signed a confidentiality agreement which forbids him to talk about this to anyone else." Fisher checks his watch again, rises from the table, and heads for the door. "Thank you both for coming."

"Why did you close the factory?" Cassie shouts after him.

Fisher turns, saving his smuggest smile for last.

"Cassie, Goetia owns hundreds of companies and premises all over the world. We open and close them every day. The Avonfield site just wasn't viable any more."

"Rubbish! That factory's been there for a hundred years! You didn't need to close it now."

The assembled Goetia gathering stand quickly and surge towards the exit in an almost undignified rush.

Cassie grinds her teeth.

We shake hands with Parkes and leave the room, venturing out onto Euston Road via the building's cavernous lobby and spotless revolving doors.

"Waste of time," mutters Cassie. "All of it."

At Paddington, I order a big cup of the strongest coffee available, but it's still not enough to disguise the acrid taste of the latest tablets.

Cassie and I buy a paper and decide to spend the trip home tackling the cryptic crossword, the theory being that it will distract me from the Trespassers.

It works for a good hour until things take a sickening turn for the worse.

As the train draws into Swindon, I see Weeper seated forlornly on a bench, tears streaming from his baggy eyes. I gaze upon this sad spectacle and feel a sudden, desperate pity for him. He's certainly not the worst of the bunch.

As we pull away, he stands bolt upright and raises his fists to the sky.

"Help me!" he yells above the din of our departing train.

My bladder loosens, and I look at Cassie in a blind panic.

"What's the matter? Who have you seen?"

"It's not who I've seen. It's what I've heard."

We transfer from the train to the bus when we arrive at Bath, leaving the rush hour traffic behind as we head out towards the tranquillity of Avonfield.

I spend the journey in a frightened daze. Cassie suggests I call Randall when we get home.

He sounds lousy.

We discuss his trip to Goetia last week, compare pill colours (his are also blue it seems), and which Trespassers he's seeing (he calls them "Weeds"). He is also spotting new ones on a regular basis, and he says that he's seen his nemesis, Gangland, already this week. He tells me that he actually appeared at Goetia, resting his polished brogues on the table, fixing Randall with his manic stare as he trimmed his finger-nails with a flick-knife.

He says things "aren't that great" at the moment. I'm guessing that means some sort of trouble with his wife Kim or his employers. I hope it's something else, but neither of them struck me as being particularly supportive. I consider relaying the latest, grim revelation at Swindon, but it sounds like he's got more than enough on his plate.

I suggest a walk out to the factory tomorrow morning, if nothing else to see if confronting it will some how steel our resolve. He says it can't hurt.

Randall waits on the corroded iron footbridge, the same graffitied eyesore that we've used as a meeting place since we were children. He peers across the fields of early morning haze, towards the razor-wired fortress of the factory. Alarmingly, he puffs on a small, hand-rolled cigarette and I realise now how difficult a go he's having.

He presents me a weary smile.

"Nice day for it," he says.

He proffers a tin of pre-rolled cigarettes, but I decline.

"I thought you'd given those up in college, mate."

"Needs must and all that bollocks," he says, gazing back towards the steel chimney and the huddle of Victorian brick buildings surrounding it.

"How's Cassie?" he asks, snapping from his fugue.

"Alright, thanks. She's taken her mum shopping today. How about Kim?"

"Not a happy bunny, mate, to be honest. She's struggling with all of this big time. Not that I blame her, of course."

"Sorry to hear that," I reply, wishing there was something more comforting I could say.

"Shall we?" he asks, flicking the remnants of his cigarette into the swollen river below.

"Why not?"

We cross the bridge and hike down the slippery steps to the riverbank. The sodden autumn grass soaks the cuffs of my old jeans, and I silently curse myself for wearing my best shoes instead of something more appropriate. The river crawls past like a huge grey glacier, a far cry from the serene summer flow when Randall and I fished here.

He lights up another cigarette as we stroll.

The quiet is shattered when a motorboat buzzes past. A woollen-hatted captain holds a steaming, red mug in one hand and makes minute adjustments to the wheel with the other. A few months ago, its irritating drone would have scattered the ducks, but not anymore. They've gone the same way as the fish and the moorhens.

"Look at—"

Randall stops mid-sentence, eyes frozen on the boat, and I glance down at the cigarette smouldering in his trembling hand. I know that reaction.

"Which one?" I ask solemnly.

"Gangland. Standing in the back of the boat… It's that stare. I just can't handle it."

Randall looks beaten.

"I can hear them now, you know," he says.

"Me too," I say, but my reply doesn't register.

As the boat chugs out of sight, he puts the cigarette to his lips and draws on it until the blackening paper burns his fingers.

"Fuck!" he cries, throwing the stub to the ground.

As we continue walking, I remember the last time we fished here. I couldn't easily forget it. A glorious summer evening, hoisting perch from the river, a case of beer set invitingly on the bank. I recall his puzzled expression as the clear surface of the water slowly took on a coppery sheen, a rainbow-patterned slick spreading out from the edges. A caustic mist hung over the spill, drifting towards us and making us sick.

We came back the following day and found the usual anglers and dog walkers replaced by a team of hi-vis suits, wearing facemasks and scooping fish carcasses from the river.

The riverbank terminates as we reach the factory's perimeter. We stand side by side and peer through the wire mesh at the familiar old buildings, which are now not only shuttered but sealed for good measure. The workers may have gone, but there's still movement here—a small black CCTV camera swivels in our direction.

Randall spits through the fence in its direction.

"Bastards," he mutters. "They'll pay for this one way or the other. I'm going to give that clown Parkes another month, then I'm going to the papers."

"What about the confidentially agreement?" I ask.

He nearly chokes in disgust.

"Confidentially agreement? How many others are out there, keeping quiet in return for a nice little payoff? Half the village, I reckon. Have you been in The Crown lately?"

He doesn't wait for an answer.

"It's empty. They're all sitting at home going out of their tiny minds, waiting for some juicy compensation offer that's never going to come."

"I think you're being a bit paranoid, mate. We were the only ones by the river that night. As far as we know, it's only us that—"

"Wake up!" he roars. "I've already lost my job, and my marriage is rowing up shit creek. And those fuckers are trying to sweep it all under the carpet!"

In a fit of rage that would make Choler proud, Randall digs his pill bottle from his coat pocket and launches it over the fence onto the factory grounds.

I know him well enough than to try and reason with him when he's like this, so I turn and walk back towards the bridge. Randall trails behind me, and we complete the journey in awkward silence.

At the bridge, he turns towards me, crestfallen.

"Sorry mate, no offence," he says.

The look on his face breaks my heart. I look back at him with all the seriousness I can muster.

"None taken. Twat."

He smiles at me, the famous Randall smile of old, and gives me a big, tobacco-scented hug.

I heave an inward sigh of disappointment when Cassie suggests we spend the evening watching *Les Misérables*. I really can't imagine it being my cup of tea, but the DVD's been lying there since her birthday, and the past week has made me realise how much I've taken her for granted. I brace myself with the three essentials of a Saturday night: our cat Pedro purring on my lap, a freshly uncorked bottle of Shiraz, and a vast array of savoury snacks.

To my surprise, I find myself engrossed in the movie, and at the end of the evening I fall into bed and drift off into a semi-contented sleep.

A distant cacophony rouses me at three o'clock.

I head groggily into the living room, assuming Cassie's left the television on, but it sits dark and mute in the corner. Pedro blinks drowsily at me before yawning and collapsing back into a furry brown heap.

I peer out the window at the student's house across the road, but only see a wall of dim lights behind drawn curtains.

My gaze wanders up to a row of neatly parked cars, and there, bathed in the orange sodium glare of the street lamps, is Kallix.

She leans against a black VW Beetle as discordant guitar riffs and strangled vocals pour from its open windows. The perfect soundtrack to my waking nightmare. It's a shame I can't trade Trespassers with Randall; this music is much more up his alley. Her eyes closed in some hypnotic rapture, Kallix bobbles her head in slow loops.

I dash to the kitchen, grab the milk carton from the fridge, and use it to wash down two more of the bitter tablets. The music still shatters the normal silence of the street below. I think about calling Kallix's bluff and marching out to confront her. They can't touch me after all. In one of my more frustrated moments, I'd once swung a drunken punch at Slammer, but it simply passed through him and I tumbled onto the pavement.

I reach the door when I decide against confrontation. I'm not sure the sight of me shouting at thin air in the middle of the night would particularly impress the neighbours.

Fetching the spare duvet from the airing cupboard, I tramp back to the living room and lie down on the sofa. I pull the duvet over my head and press my palms against my ears until I hear nothing except my own racing heartbeat.

Cassie enters the lounge on Sunday morning, and she spies my bloodshot eyes and the little notebook open on the coffee table.

"Jesus," she says, flinching at my appearance. "What happened?"

I tell her about the musical interlude during the night.

"Why didn't you wake me?"

"What for? What's the point in two of us having our sleeps disturbed?"

She slumps her shoulders, powerless. She plods into the kitchen and flicks the kettle on, returning three minutes later with two full mugs and an instant change in attitude.

"Right. This is getting ridiculous. Get on the phone with Parkes tomorrow morning. Those pills you're on now are useless. You can't wait another month for the next lot. Not that they'll be any better. But at least it's something you can do for yourself."

I shrug. I tell her I'll call him first thing in the morning.

Now I've just got today to deal with.

The revelation of sound has added an extra, unwanted dimension to my days. Seeing the Trespassers was never particularly pleasant, but their total lack of sound made them easy to pick out, and seemed to blunt much of the implicit menace they posed.

The lovely golden sky of the previous morning has been replaced by a slate blanket that wraps the village in a dour drizzle. Cassie recommends we try to stay positive and make the most of the day. I'm not overjoyed at her suggestion of a walk to Wrekin's Folly but, as I have as much chance of bumping into the Trespassers in my bathroom as I do in the woods, I figure I don't have much to lose.

I tug on my boots by the doorstep, knocking free the caked mud from my last excursion into the forest. We leave.

Things start off agreeable enough until Choler shows his ugly face, gripping a rope swing with one hand while shaking his fist dementedly with the other. I do my best to ignore him.

As we pass The Crown, I ponder Randall's outburst. Is it really just us, or are there others? What did they put into the river? Was it even Goetia's doing?

A young couple waits for us to pass through the kissing gate that leads into the woods. A huge, straggly wolfhound stands behind them, clenching a gnawed stick proudly in its drooling jaws. I smell the sweet tinge of marijuana, mixed with the damp, musty odour of the dog.

The girl giggles and wishes us a cheery "good morning," but I can sense my paranoia kicking in. Is there something strange about that smile? Why isn't he smiling? Are they both actually there, or is one of them some dark freeloader, hijacking a Sunday dog walk? As they amble away, I crane my neck to make sure they're out of sight, then ask Cassie how many people we had just happened upon.

"Two," she answers.

I feel the worry evaporate from my mind and I grasp Cassie's hand, resolving to try and enjoy the remainder of our stroll for both our sakes.

"Ah, the sweet innocence of youth," I say, jollier already. "Strange choice of dog for a couple like that, though."

Cassie stops in her tracks.

"What dog?" she asks.

Our jaunt to Wrekin's Folly otherwise goes smoothly enough. The trees explode in rust, gold, and crimson, a final defiant burst of colour before their inevitable surrender to winter. Cassie, enthralled, snaps pictures with her phone.

Perhaps I'll be able to appreciate the autumn glory of these trees one day, rather than wondering who's about to peek out from behind them.

After an hour's steady uphill climb, we reach a barren plateau which presents us stunning views of the village below and the weathered husk of the Folly. The ancient tower teeters heavenward into the low-hanging clouds. I step back and follow the cracked brickwork up into the murk. A gust of wind briefly clears the sky, and then I see him.

My knees nearly buckle. Crooked Head squats in the stone window frame at the top of the tower, glaring straight down at me.

I can hear Cassie talking to me, but she might as well be inside the tower.

My mind spins, feverishly struggling to understand why he fills me with so much dread, and then I know. Despite his twisted neck, which seems unable to hold the weight of his head upright, his face looks perfectly normal. Perhaps no more than twenty years of age, he's dressed the same as any man in the village. The irony is, he scares me so much because he's the only one that doesn't do anything. The others have their own surreal routines, but he sits motionless. His size doesn't help—he must be at least 6' 4"—but it's his sheer calmness that represents more of a threat than the rest of them put together.

In a moment of pure instinctive panic, I seize Cassie by the hand, and we hurry back through the woods, hitting a full run through the slush of fallen leaves.

I phone Parkes on Monday morning and tell him that I'm hearing and smelling things now. He says he'll do what he can.

He calls me back an hour later and, to my relief, informs me that Goetia would be more than happy to see me whenever I'm available, even this afternoon if it's convenient.

I call Cassie at her job and tell her that I can be in London by three o'clock if public transport is running on schedule. She asks me if I want her to finish up by lunch so that she can join me. I tell her that she's taken more than enough time off already, and that I'll be fine.

"Good luck," she says. "And don't forget your pills."

To my pleasant surprise, the bus, train, and tube rides are all Trespasser-free, but as I enter the meeting room at Goetia, I immediately notice things are different. The assembled group is much smaller than usual, which is understandable as some of the regular psychiatrists and chemists must be flown in from all over the place, judging by their accents.

Parkes is already seated at the table, appearing as bemused as I feel.

"Have a chair, Jack, and thanks for coming at such short notice," says Fisher, already in top condescending form. "Well, I'll cut to the chase," he continues after I sit. "We've decided to settle, if that's okay with you."

Parkes looks at me, and I can't tell which of us is more shocked.

"Goetia still believes that it's done nothing wrong, but we'd like get this whole business out of the way once and for all."

He slides across a thick wedge of paperwork, and I skim the miniscule font on the front sheet. It looks like the standard legal tosh until I see, highlighted on the bottom of the page in larger lettering, the words *Five Hundred Thousand Pounds*.

"I hope you'll find it's an acceptable sum for all your, um, problems. Take your time. Discuss it with your legal people, and Cassie, obviously. Just let us know if, and when, you'd be willing to sign. I needn't remind you that the confidentiality clause remains in place."

I nod, but I'm not really taking all this in.

"Obviously that only covers the financial remuneration. The chemists will continue to work full time on your case until you're completely recovered, but I think it's fair to say with this batch we're pretty much there."

"I think we need time to study this," mumbles Parkes while slipping the documents into his briefcase.

I nod in agreement.

"Of course. Take as long as you need."

As we rise to leave, a rotund, white-coated man shambles around the table to present me with yet another bottle of pills.

"Ah, good man," smiles Fisher at the sheepish chemist.

To my slight disappointment, the tablets are plain white.

I march through the shining lobby and out into the gleaming city. The rumbling buses idle patiently in the snarled traffic, but the chaos of early-evening London has never looked so beautiful. I walk down Euston Street until the Goetia building is out of sight, then punch the air in utter delight.

I need to phone Cassie, but it's too noisy here, and I also need a few minutes to compose myself.

A mini-mart offers a tempting range of beverages with which to celebrate. I consider buying a bottle of champagne, but as I'm not out of the proverbial woods yet I settle on a can of premium lager. I pop it open as I head towards the tube station, washing down one of the new snow-white pills. It tastes wonderful—a tangy blend of oranges and apricots.

I locate a quiet alleyway to ring Cassie. When I fish my mobile from my pocket I see I've missed three calls, all from Randall. A text message reads "CALL ME NOW."

My mood plummets suddenly. I knew him dumping all those pills over the fence was a serious mistake.

"Where the fuck have you been?" he demands when he picks up.

"London. I've just been to see Goetia. And listen, mate, things are looking up," I gush, but I can feel my euphoria already withering.

"Huh?" He sounds confused. "You were in there just last week. I thought your appointments were once a fortnight?"

"I can't say too much now, but the money's sorted."

"Eh?"

"They've settled. At long bloody last, they've settled. The end is nigh, mate."

"Did they give you any more pills?" he asks.

"Yes. Could be the final batch, they said. Guess which colour—"

"Have you taken any?" he interjects.

"Just the one."

"Shit."

I can hear him take a nervous draw on a cigarette.

"Chuck them. Chuck them right now. Throw the fucking things in the Thames!"

"What?"

"Remember Saturday?"

I certainly do.

"Any guess what's happened since?"

Here we go.

"Nothing," he says.

I'm grappling to fathom this.

"Absolutely fuck all," he adds. "I haven't seen anything since Gangland on the stern of that boat. Don't you get it?"

"Not really," I say.

"That shit in the river was just the beginning. We've been taken for a ride. It's been those goddamned tablets all along. Screwing with our heads."

My brain frantically seeks the right words to reply with, but comes up blank.

I switch my phone off.

I trudge dejectedly down into the bowels of the Underground, oblivious to the people hurtling past me. As I reach the platform, a scything pain flames across my gut, and I crumple to the floor in agony.

The pain eventually recedes, and I open my rheumy eyes to a deserted concrete wilderness.

Why did nobody help me? I check my watch. I'd only blacked out for a few minutes.

The board tells me the next train is approaching and I hope I can at least make it as far as Paddington before anything else affects me.

I peer into the tunnel until the faint lights of the oncoming tube appear.

Moments later it emerges from the darkness, and I see the lopsided silhouette of Crooked Head sitting stock-still in the driver's seat.

As the train creeps to a halt, I look into the carriage and there they all are: Choler, Kallix, Drench, Weeper, and a sinister parade of others, all staring in my direction.

"Mind the gap," booms a cold voice from the ceiling above me, as the doors part and I am beckoned inside.

Beauty Is Skin

Daniel Hale

"The Lady has heard your plea, madam." The girl who had told me this was just another white-shirted assistant to the Thai face-masseuse I'd been seeing in Beverly Hills. I'd never given her a second glance before, but now she stood over me on the lift chair and pressed a card into my hand.

"Seek her out," she whispered in a dreamy, reverential tone. "She will aid you."

It was a plain white card. No embossments, just a phone number written in red pen. I tucked it into my purse, telling myself that I was just humoring a poor emigrant. I didn't want to admit to myself that I already had an idea what the girl was talking about.

I had a problem, you see, but I wouldn't acknowledge it. By the age of fifty I had done just about every conceivable thing necessary to become Somebody.

In my younger days I'd been the leading lady in the top romance films of the century. None of that sentimental teenage trash you see nowadays, boy meets girl, formulaic nonsense. No, mine were *tragedies*, searing testaments to the deprecations of the heart. Nothing you'd ever see today.

Even when I hit my forties, and my perfect cheekbones and flawless cream skin were marked with crow's feet and wrinkles, I still had the sultry appeal of a jaded yet hungry older woman. I had passion still to spare. In *The Final Lotus* I was the very image of an elegant femme fatale, corrupting the young hero with every ounce of class I had. Men were drooling over me in the theaters while their women fumed and longed.

Now those same men are stepping over me on the sidewalk when I can't bother to move anymore. Those same women look away, or toss me the odd dollar. Disgust I could almost deal with. Being unseen is unbearable. Pity? Pity is the worst of all.

I divorced three husbands: a sitcom dad, a pharmaceuticals magnate, and a talk show host. In each case I walked away with more money than I knew what to do with, so I hired people to help me spend it in the mostly publicly impressive ways possible. Sports cars and limos. Designer clothes. Lavish vacations to the Bahamas, Italy, Brazil. Plastic surgery.

Eventually the last thing my agent could arrange for me was a reality TV show. I stuck with it for a while, but inside I knew it was the end, the ultimate indignity for a Hollywood star. There's no part to play as yourself, and when you have to fake even that you know the show is over. I thought I could give it up with some semblance of dignity and just retire to enjoy my wealth in peace.

I should have realized that it was too late for me. But I loved being in the spotlight, and I was terrified of being shoved out of it. More than that, I loved the thrill of chasing after the next treatment, the next trend, the next discovery that would make me stand out from the crowd, the more exotic the better.

I must have had a dozen procedures done. I restructured my face so many times I no longer recognized myself in the mirror. I changed hair color, grew it down to my waist, then shaved it all off. I went to fashion shows and movie premieres in the most outrageous outfits I could find. I once attended a performance of *La Traviata* at the Sydney Opera House with my hair molded into a perfect replica of it.

Did the Lady recognize in me the desperation to be noticed? Did my antics amuse her? Or did she simply see in me the resources she needed? It doesn't matter. The end result is that I went to her. She laid the bait and I took it greedily. And for my troubles she hollowed me out and made me this cold husk of a person, a wicked-looking hag. My hair is dried straw that falls out every morning, and my skin is creased, faded parchment, devoid of the tan I'd spent so much time and money cultivating.

Everything hurts so much now. The rags I've covered myself in are no comfort, every breeze grates across my skin like razor blades. And every time someone goes out of their way to *not* see me is a stab to my chest far worse than anything I could have imagined.

She took everything that ever mattered to me, and left nothing but the memory.

For two weeks I ignored the plain card that sat in the bottom of my purse, but I kept remembering the look in the girl's eyes, the whisper of her voice, a messenger from the Divine.

It nagged at me.

I finally snapped one night after a charity ball, when that whore who did those lipstick commercials told me that she could hardly notice the gray in my hair. It was a trial not to claw the little wench's sparkling eyes out.

So the minute I got home I grabbed the phone and dialed the number.

One ring. Two. Finally somebody picked up and an effeminate male voice spoke.

"How can I help you, ma'am?"

"I, um… How did you know I was a woman?"

"Oh, we have been expecting your call for a while now, madam. It's quite an honor. I just *loved* you in that movie with De Niro." The mellowness of the voice held a hint of condescension, and I flushed with embarrassment. "What can the Lady do for you?"

"This *lady* is some kind of practitioner?"

"She is a saint, madam. An artist. All that lives is like clay beneath her fingers. She is a magus that defies the forces of nature. Skin, scale, chitin—all bend to her will and blend for her as one."

I snorted, feeling on firmer ground. "So I'm expected to pay good money for some kind of self-professed holistic shaman? Or should it be sham?"

"Oh dear, the Lady is no fraud. And as in most things in life, her price is only as great as you're willing to pay."

"Well, forgive me if I'm unwilling to take beauty tips from some anonymous 'Lady' who sounds more like a cult leader than a plastic surgeon. Can I at least have a name? Where does she practice?"

"She is reluctant to divulge such details to prospective clients." He spoke slowly, as one would to a particularly dense child.

"Her methods are not… widely performed. It's all extremely confidential. There is a severe risk of infringement in this industry, and she prefers to meet new clients on her own ground. There are spies everywhere, you see."

"Really." I tried to sound uninterested, though my skin was tensing with frustration. "Then it seems we won't be doing business. I know all about spies. They all work for the media. Thanks anyway."

"I'm very sorry to hear that," he matched me my uninterested and raised it to outright boredom. "The Lady is of course sympathetic, which is why she utilizes private facilities to discuss business. Rest assured that these meetings are highly discreet, and believe me when I say that you will find it quite impossible to pull yourself away once you see what she has to offer."

Again, there was the desire to just let this alone. The entire operation sounded so shady, and I was fearful of compromising my dimming but still enduring image. But again I felt the pull of something, like an answered prayer. The edge I desired.

At last I gave my consent.

I was given an address in the slummier part of town. I was told to come alone. I would be approached.

"How can I be sure that this isn't some kind of con?"

"You can't," was the reply. "But then, that applies to most things."

I didn't like the idea of taking my own car to such a neighborhood, so I walked downtown and took a bus from there.

I put on a heavy black trench coat and sunglasses, and a floral scarf over my hair. That was more for my ego's benefit than any worries that somebody would recognize me. I felt rather like an adulteress off to meet her suitor in some run-down motel. The bus driver looked worried when I told him where I was going, and cautioned me to get home safe.

The address belonged to the seediest bar I've ever seen. The words 'HOT ROCKET' flashed in red neon above the door, while something loud and rhythmic thundered and shook the broken glass on the sidewalk.

Inside, the walls were covered with concert posters and magazine ads for bands I'd never heard of. Most of them seemed to tend towards bare-chested men with long, sweaty hair sporting electric guitars and angry expressions. The only illumination was strings of Christmas lights hanging in hap-hazard jumbles from the corners.

A smattering of customers sat drinking at mismatched tables, occasionally glancing at a makeshift stage in the far corner where a bare-chested young man with long, sweaty hair strummed his electric guitar and screamed into a micro-phone. The music was too harsh for me to understand the lyrics. I went to the bar and shouted for a soda water.

"We only serve beer, honey," the barmaid replied, raising her voice above the din. She looked young enough to be my daughter, but regarded me like I was a lost child who had wandered in by accident.

I asked for whatever she recommended, and she gave me a bottle with a picture of a smiling devil flipping me off.

I took a table in the rear, sipping my drink and trying not to gag. I expected that at any moment some rough, greasy biker would sidle up and proposition me for something lewd and unseemly.

But as I glanced around I realized most of the stares I attracted were more out of curiosity than malice. One man met my eyes and shook his head.

"Good evening."

I looked at the woman standing before me. Auburn hair fell in ringlets around her brown, heart-shaped face. She was wearing big dark sunglasses and a red scarf around her neck, and a white topcoat that reached her ankles. She smiled a warm, dimpled smile.

I found myself liking her instantly.

"You must be the Lady," I said.

She laughed a bubbly, pretty laugh. "I'm afraid not. I'm the Lady's representative. I interview prospective clients for their suitability to receive her services."

"And what constitutes suitability, precisely?"

"Oh, a number of things." Her smile widened. "But it's best to discuss such matters in private. Please follow me."

She led me past the bar and through a bead-curtained door. It was pitch dark, and the woman held my hand to guide me.

For a moment we paused. I spotted a small, blue light flicker on the wall in front of me, and heard a deep clicking followed by a loud thud. A vault-like door swung open into a dimly lit white room. I blinked to adjust my sight and surveyed our surroundings. Just a bare space with subdued overhead fluorescents. Nothing else that I could see.

"This is a meeting room?" I asked.

"More of a showcase."

The woman removed her sunglasses. Her eyes were pale turquoise completely through, iris *and* pupil. They gleamed like blue marbles. I wondered if she was blind.

"The Lady prefers to show prospective clients what they have the opportunity to buy."

Slowly, she untied her scarf and displayed her neck. Her skin was covered in elegant swirls of rich crimson and mauve, spiraling down from her ears and meeting at the collarbone, with ember tongues branching off and around and down to her shoulders. They appeared to glow faintly from within, and as I watched the glow seemed to *move*, waning in places and brightening in others.

She unbuttoned her coat and shrugged it off. She was completely naked, and her body was adorned with more of the bioluminescent patterns. Drops of blue light seemed to trickle between her breasts, while more ripples of mauve and scarlet flowed and bled across her arms and legs.

But her waist was what most caught my attention. The skin was transparent, like a thin plastic bag. There were no organs visible, but I could see her spine curving up and away in the back.

I saw tiny beads of emerald-like light shine into being. Dark green and blue butterflies clutched the woman's spine, waving their phosphorescent wings languidly. All of a sudden they took off, fluttering about her insides and creating hypnotic neon whorls.

My heart was thumping in my mouth, and my sweat was icy cold. Trembling, I laid a hand on the woman's midriff. She shivered at my touch. It felt like the smoothest skin imaginable, and my fingers brushed along the trails of light.

"The Lady chooses her clients carefully," she whispered. "She wants nothing more than to help the beautiful realize their potential. But she defies nature. She defies evolution and symmetry. There are those who do not look at such genius kindly. Only those fully willing to change may take the risk to receive her gift."

"Risk?"

"There is always a risk."

Then she placed her palm against my cheek. "You should know this. Beauty never comes cheaply. The Lady will take what she is owed once she has finished with you. Do you consent?"

I stared into her beautiful, jeweled eyes and nodded. She smiled, and leaned down to me.

The time I spent in that room, exploring every inch of the woman's modifications, was a blur. More than once I'm sure the entire affair went beyond talking business. Yet I was in the grip of something. I felt dizzy, drugged. I could only liken it to some spiritual ritual, inhaling hallucinogenic vapors to contact a higher power. Here was my desire—ultimate beauty—all for my own, and I only had to say that I wanted it.

I remembered little after that. A limousine taking me home, and the glowing woman sitting in front of me, still naked and smiling.

When I woke up there was another card on my bedside table, with another address, an intersection. It instructed me to be there at midnight.

It said, "You will be collected."

It was drizzling when I was picked up from a bus shelter. I was again in my adulteress getup. I felt cold and jittery, paranoid. I kept glancing at the elderly woman sitting next to me on the bench. She seemed to be sleeping. I found myself wondering why such an old woman would be out so late, until I told myself to calm down.

When the limo showed up, I sprinted to it as fast as my heels would allow. I was disappointed to find that the glowing woman wasn't there with me, but I was glad about the liquor cabinet. I poured myself a scotch and sat back, trying to soothe my rapidly fraying nerves. The divider to the front seat was up, and I didn't see a switch to slide it down. I wondered if it was an ordinary human being driving me, or another adherent of the Lady's processes, another sample of living art.

We couldn't have been driving for more than half an hour when we stopped. A voice—presumably the driver's—

spoke from an intercom I hadn't noticed before. "We have arrived, ma'am. Please walk straight through the green door directly in front of you upon exiting." The voice had a very mechanical tone to it.

I stepped out of the limo, my skin prickling again. Nerves. A flickering streetlight illuminated a row of tenement houses, dull gray brick walls pockmarked with boarded-over windows and rusty fire escapes. Most of the doors were a dirty white, but the one right before me was an incongruous lime green. I did not give myself the option of hesitating. I marched right up to it and entered.

Shuddering, I closed the door behind me and leaned against it. My breathing quickened. There was a tungsten light bulb above me and shadows down the hall. Nothing else.

A minute passed. Then another. And another. I thought I could make out movement in the shadows, felt eyes on me.

Finally they stepped forward—twin sisters, or women so alike that it made no difference. Each had pale yellow skin, like jaundice. Each had coal black hair reaching down to their waists in identical plaits. Each had rose tattoos, the thorned stems swirling down their arms and curling over their bodies. They were both dressed like belly dancers, with sheer silvery sarongs enwrapping their legs and spangling bra tops of black and gold.

They both possessed a third arm—overlong and double-jointed, swinging back and forth—growing from between their shoulder blades.

I steeled myself, refusing now to show the same awed sycophancy I had before. They didn't seem too impressed.

"The Lady will see you." They spoke together, in voices so quiet they sounded like a single person.

Something was wrong. I know that now, and I think I could have known it then. If only I hadn't been trying so hard to clamp down my fear, denying the things that didn't add up—the late night pickup, the empty street, for god's sake, the simple fact that I'd *never* before seen anyone like the Lady's treated adherents. All I could think about was being remade into a goddess: wondrous, alien, terrifying, and beautiful all at once. I was *drunk* with desire, desperate beyond reason.

Never mind the questions, never mind the mysteries.

I needed this!

Did I half-expect it when the Sisters grabbed me by the arms? I succumbed so easily to their hold, and yes, it was only a hold. They didn't grip or restrain me, but supported me like I'd had a few too many and were escorting me to the bedroom to sleep it off.

It wasn't until their third arms reached around from behind them and covered my face that I thought to struggle. It didn't last.

Suddenly their palms seemed to soften and liquefy, flesh becoming wet putty while a sharp scent filled my nostrils. I felt heavy and light all at once, unable to resist as they propped me up and dragged me into the darkness.

How much of it can I believe? How much of it was a hallucination brought about by the Sisters' organic drug?

That massive stone chamber, murkily lit by a gigantic chandelier, seemed real enough, though it rocked so alarmingly. I was kneeling, pushed down by the twins. A woman stood in front of me and lifted my chin, turning my head this way and that, examining me. The antlers sticking up from her head seemed more like tree branches, ornamented with purple buds and tiny, wispy birds. They chittered softly, hopping from branch to branch, never leaving the circumference of the woman's head.

"Quite the withered old bitch, isn't she?" The woman spoke in a high-class English accent and sneered at me. The drugs were making me muzzy, and I'm sure I looked pitiable. "Not much left in her I should think, the poor cow. Honestly, the Lady will have her hands full finding anything salvageable in this wretch."

"Where… where's…" My mouth felt stuffed with cotton, and I swallowed, trying to form the words. "The Lady, where is…"

"Why, she's right in front of you, dear."

The woman gestured grandly toward the far side of the chamber. An enormous pile of velvet ropes appeared to be coiled there, but I had trouble making out much more than that. I stood up, swaying. The ropes seemed to squirm about each other, falling away from some central mass that was gradually rising.

Then my brain registered what my eyes were beholding: a kraken was materializing from the shadows, and I didn't have the strength or presence of mind to flee from it.

A blood red limb—slick and slithery, covered in tiny suction cups—shot out and wrapped around my torso. I struggled drunkenly, scarcely noting the sharp pain like millions of fishhooks digging into my flesh. The tentacle brought me up to the top of the heap.

The figure of a woman with porcelain skin, nude and lithe, jutted from the writhing mass. Her striking face was perfectly made up, with dead gray eyes and full red lips smiling cruelly at me. Her own hair was composed of tentacles, wound upon her head into a stunning beehive.

The Lady waved to me, fingers waggling playfully. I still sat there, clasped in her tentacle and moaning, no longer sure of anything around me. Only when the Lady pulled the mask away to reveal her true face did I finally scream. I knew I was in a nightmare now, and I screamed my lungs out as the monster's puckered toothy mouth drew closer, opening wide.

I fought, even as the Lady pulled me into her folds and the real pain began.

The scars fit, don't they? All along my arms, these little red scabs, like thousands of needle pricks. She stung me with something, I know that. I could feel myself being drained of vitality, of color, of fat, of life, whatever the Lady could use.

There's not a mention of me in any of the papers. I get copies from the bins. Nobody remembers me at all. The others are still there, still mugging their hollow smiles for the cameras, in their fetching gowns and coiffed hair. She has all of them marked for recycle, I'm sure.

This is the cruelest thing she could have done. I suffer no doubts about her abilities now. I'm certain she could rip the very neurons from my brain to boost the wit of some other dazzling socialite. She could have stripped me of my sense completely and left me a helpless invalid, squatting in a trashcan and soiling myself. She could have, but it was much more satisfying to leave me my mind, so I could see how far I'd fallen.

The Lady doesn't advertise. She doesn't need to. She doesn't require patrons or admirers. She seeks out her adherents carefully, her dedicated volunteers ready and willing to be remade into living works of art. She doesn't need anyone to tell her how good she is. Her medium is flesh, and she seeks out her donors with even more care. We're ideal for her, the devout celebrities. People famous just for being famous. We shine so brightly in the limelight, hoping to outshine all the others and blind with our fire.

Who's going to notice when one star disappears from a sea of so many others?

We burn as brightly as we can, until all that's left is the light. Even as we flicker and die, the light remains, and nobody thinks to look beyond it.

The Silence
of Hestia

Paul Starkey

The doctors had lied. They'd said rousing from the effects of suspension would be no different from awakening from a night's sleep. What they'd evidently meant, Imogen realized now, was getting up after a loud, tequila-fuelled evening.

The lights in the chamber were dim, but still she kept her eyes shut, one hand draped across them as she just lay there in her open sarcophagus.

Her head pounded, a deep throbbing bass in sync with her heart, both beats steadily increasing as full consciousness returned.

She knew she had to rise. She felt so tired though. Amazing that one could feel so fatigued after so much sleep.

With a groan she opened her eyes a crack and reached up with both hands to grip the cold sides of the sarcophagus. After a moment she grunted and levered herself up into a sitting position.

Imogen shivered. She knew something was amiss, but the faux hangover had dulled her senses, so it took a few seconds to realize what was wrong. In the end it wasn't the obvious things, wasn't the fact that the lights were down too low, or that several of the suspension pods around her were dark, whilst far too many still glowed from within.

No, it was none of these. It was the absence of Hestia's soothing voice in her mind. It had been there before she'd slipped into her long sleep, and it should have been there now that she was awake. An ongoing faint litany, most of it chaotic, strings of numbers interspersed with the occasional word or phrase. She was linked to Hestia. They all were, able to instantaneously communicate with the ship's AI at a moment's notice.

That Hestia's algorithmic song had fallen silent bespoke a problem far greater than any they'd anticipated.

Sitting up had made Imogen feel dizzy, and the zero-g was not helping. She closed her eyes again and took deep breaths. Eventually she opened them once more.

"Hestia? Hestia, respond?"

She didn't need to say the words. The thought would have been enough, but habits died hard. This was why she tended to look upwards whenever she addressed the AI as well. Alicia always laughed at this.

"She isn't a real goddess, and she isn't in heaven."

At the thought of her twin sister, Imogen looked to her left, at the sarcophagus three along from her own. It was dark, though those in-between still glowed. Imogen frowned. Too many questions and she felt too shitty to work out answers to them.

She carefully clambered out of her sarcophagus, wishing she could stop thinking of it like that. It'd started out an amusing joke amongst many of the pilgrims, but most had tired of it. Imogen was one of the few who still referred to the cryogenic suspension pods with some variation of the word 'coffin'.

The deck was cold when her bare feet touched it, so she let herself drift upwards, holding tight to the sides of her pod so she did not float away. She cast her gaze around the chamber once more. Assessment time. On the downside Hestia was silent, and clearly something was awry given that it looked like perhaps a dozen pods were either offline or empty, including her own. Either they should all be awake, or just a handful of those whose specialties related to ship's systems.

Imogen was a geologist.

On the upside there was still power, judging by the minimal light and heat, and the air tasted okay, so life support was functioning. Plus almost eighty pods were still working as far as she could tell.

She wasn't about to inspect every single one. She did however decide to check Alicia's. Slender posts were fixed to the floor at conveniently spaced locations, allowing you to manoeuvre around the chamber with ease despite the lack of gravity. She grabbed the nearest one and pulled herself towards it, then reached for the next, and so on, until she arrived at her sister's sarcophagus.

Pod, her mind told her. It's a pod!

Except as she leaned over it she knew that sarcophagus might be the better term, because the lid wasn't retracted as hers had been. There was a small glass window built into the lid, but it was smeared with grime.

Her headache seemed distant now, though in hindsight she preferred it to the fear that now clenched her gut. Slowly she wiped the dirt away, terrified that she was going to find her sister's desiccated corpse staring back at her.

Just a pillow.

As her stomach relaxed, her headache resumed. She did not mind the trade-off.

Okay, time to move on. She couldn't float here in her underwear all day. She needed to get to the flight deck, or at least to a computer panel in order to ascertain what was happening.

It was possible that those already awake were working on the problem—her sister was a pilot after all. Of course that still didn't explain why Imogen was awake.

A malfunction? The idea didn't sound very plausible, but she had nothing better to go on.

There was a chill in the air. Imogen drifted towards the lockers attached to the wall and grabbed a pair of grey pants and matching T-shirt, along with a pair of orange sneakers. She was only concerned with the temperature, not modesty. Training had been co-ed and close-knit. Most of the people asleep in this room had seen her naked, and vice versa.

She turned away from the locker, then crouched before jumping upward, pushing back as she did so to angle her ascent. She was aiming toward the hatch in the ceiling and, despite how crappy she felt and how long she'd been asleep, her muscle memory and exhaustive training ensured she made the trip flawlessly. She grasped the handrails along the side and swung herself up until she was lying supine, with the hatch to her left and a computer panel to her right.

She frowned. The computer was active, but lodged in dumb-mode. This wasn't just an issue with Hestia's neural interface. The AI was offline. That meant Imogen could not retrieve as much information as she needed from the computer, and what information she could get she had to dredge from the databanks because in dumb-mode the computer was neither intuitive nor speedy.

After almost twenty minutes of laborious effort just to get the bare minimum, she decided enough was enough. She'd discovered the laser fusion drive was offline. They were basically coasting and had been for some time, though the computer was sketchy about how long. Besides hers, there were eleven other non-cryogenicized life signs, which made sense based on what she had observed below, and given the engine problems did seem to suggest a repair party.

Except if that were the case why were they all in Section Zero?

The Exploration and Colonization Ship (ECS) Vesta was approximately 450 meters in length. At the rear the engines took up section E, with section D primarily deuterium and tritium tanks. Section C contained the main engineering. The suspension pods were located in Section B, along with living quarters and the flight deck. At the front of the ship was the inverted cone of section A, with storage, sensors, and the main shield designed to protect them from most interstellar detritus in their path.

Section Zero was something else entirely, and the others being there made little sense.

The easiest way to find out why was to ask them. Imogen could have activated the internal comm-system—even with

Hestia out of action it should still function—but something told her not to. Post-cryogenic hangover notwithstanding, she'd had a growing sense of disquiet since awakening, and her nagging paranoia was urging caution.

She'd ask them in person. The computer indicated no hull breeches, so she popped the hatch without a second thought. The twin halves separated smoothly, and she saw a dimly lit chute rise up into total darkness. There was a ladder secured to the interior wall and she hauled herself up by it, closing the hatch once she was all the way inside.

Feeling oddly like an old-time chimney sweep, she was glad she wasn't claustrophobic, although if she had been she wouldn't have been here. The crew of ECS Vesta, as well as her sister ships (three ahead of her, six following in her wake), had been chosen for both their physical and mental perfection. A condition like claustrophobia would have seen you cut at the initial application stage.

She didn't bother with the ladder, except as a guide, shoving off from the hatch that was now below her feet. It was exhilarating. Adrenaline was starting to compensate for the headache. She passed through several hatches until she reached the one she sought. She paused, took a deep breath, and opened it.

Above her head, stars pinpricked the black canvas. She felt her stomach flip, her hands tingle. Like being in love.

She climbed out into the service corridor, the hatch closing behind her. The corridor walls were metal, but the roof above her was convex glass.

Behind her the corridor stretched towards engineering. The view terminated in the white metal shield that protected the bulk of the ship from any engine backwash. Usually you could see a halo of light around the edge of the circular shield, an artificial aurora borealis. Not now, the disc was dark.

Imogen looked ahead, saw the blunt front end veer upwards like an artificial ski slope, and somewhere beyond that, in the murk lit only by the ghostly glimmer of a million stars, was one very distinct light—47 Ursae Majoris, a main sequence star similar in magnitude to the sun, around which orbited several gas giants and one small, slightly arid, but eminently habitable world. Their destination.

Although she hadn't been able to ascertain how much distance they'd covered in their 184 year journey, somehow Imogen knew 47 Ursae Majoris was still many light years away, and she felt a crushing loneliness as she stared out into infinity. Like most people, she'd often gazed up at a starry night and felt dwarfed, but she'd never felt as small as she did now.

The forest sweeping over her head was a welcome distraction.

Section Zero was a cylindrical torus rotating around the ship, using Vesta as its axis. Imogen smiled as the greenery moved slowly overhead. The momentum of the torus ensured that it was the only area of the ship to experience normal Earth gravity, the illusion created by the centrifugal force pushing towards the outside of the wheel. Above her she could see through its glass surface, down to the trees and plants below. This self-contained world was illuminated by rows of lights ringing the ceiling of the torus, simulating night and day with unwavering accuracy.

Various species of flora *and* fauna prospered within Section Zero—though how many generations of sheep and chickens had lived and died whilst she'd been asleep was anyone's guess. Of course it was Hestia who husbanded the plants and animals via a cohort of semi-autonomous robots, and if Hestia was offline…

Imogen frowned. The garden certainly looked alright from this angle, but did she see smoke? It was difficult to tell. The wheel rotated once every forty-five seconds, so by the time you noticed something it was already gone. It couldn't be anything serious though, because that was where the only life forms—besides her and the sleepers—were located.

The journey to the transit shaft proved uneventful. As she paused outside of the transit pod, she considered again whether to use the comm-system, and once again something intangible stopped her.

She opened the door and swam inside. There was room for six people to use the pod at once, two anchored to each of the three interior walls.

With practiced ease, she flipped herself before slipping into one of the harnesses. Though she was technically upside down, once the pod was captured by the gravity of Section Zero, 'up' would quickly become 'down'.

After she pressed the launch button nothing happened for several seconds, but this wasn't unusual. The transit shaft from the ship only aligned with the corresponding shaft inside the torus once every rotation, and then only for a few seconds, so timing was critical.

Even though she knew what to expect, the g-forces as the pod launched still caught her off guard, and she had to fight to keep from retching. The trip was mercifully quick, if jolting, especially the unnerving clunk as the pod progressed from one shaft to another.

The pod decelerated, and a fresh wave of nausea swept over Imogen as gravity took hold. The pod halted, and as her feet dropped the last few inches to the deck, her stomach followed suit. This time she couldn't keep the convulsions in check. She slapped the quick release buckle of the harness and fell to her knees just as the first heave hit her. Throwing up in zero-g was something she'd only done once and hoped to never do again. Her spasms only brought up bile. After the queasiness passed she remained there on her knees for almost a minute, slowing her breathing, calming herself down.

When the doors opened she had to squint her eyes. The light inside the torus was brighter, and judging by the glare it was close to what passed for noon here. There was nobody waiting, but it didn't take long for her to determine that something had gone very wrong.

The last time she'd been out here had been a few hours before she entered her sarcophagus, Lord knew how many years ago that was now. The base of the transit shaft had been surrounded by a narrow ring of metal decking, and behind this another circlet of mown grass before you got to the somewhat more natural environs beyond.

Imogen couldn't see the deck. It was hidden by moss and vines that snaked out from the jungle around her. The neat patch of lawn had since been invaded by a thick morass of vegetation.

Calling it overgrown didn't really do it justice. Out of control would've been a better description, and she guessed it had been a long while since any of Hestia's little robots had tended this garden.

She saw a small glint of light reflecting from within a nearby tangle of branches. She moved hesitantly towards it, wary as she stepped between vines—she couldn't shake the feeling that the foliage might come alive and snatch her at any moment, dragging her further into the forest where some humongous Venus flytrap had evolved to eat human-sized flies.

She smiled. Stupid imagination.

She knelt and pushed away several branches until she could see the pint-sized robot, its once shiny carapace rusted now, its lifeless sensors resembling the sad eyes of a puppy. She felt a curious sense of pity for it.

She looked up. The vegetation rose several meters into the air, in some places much higher, and from the peak of one towering pine, needled tendrils swayed upwards towards the sky. The tree had grown so tall its topmost boughs were no longer prisoners of gravity.

It still didn't make sense. Hestia was out of commission, yet all the lights in Section Zero still worked, and clearly the sprinkler system continued to simulate rainfall, even if the brownish tinge to much of the foliage suggested it was having a tough time keeping pace with the forest's rampant spread.

Imogen rushed to the transit shaft and circled around to the rear of it. The small pedestal was there as expected, though the computer interface was dark. Undoubtedly it was still in operation since there were indentations in the mossy undergrowth to suggest someone had recently stood here. When she touched the screen it sprang to life.

She did not get a chance to analyze it, because at that moment a cry rang out from somewhere in the distance.

Imogen left the computer and returned to the front of the shaft. Her mouth had gone dry. The cry had come from somewhere inside the forest. It had plainly been human—a woman—but it hadn't been remotely intelligible.

She suddenly felt very vulnerable, alone, unarmed, and with no clue what was going on. She hugged herself. It wasn't at all cold inside the torus, yet still she felt gooseflesh beneath her fingertips. Aside from the cry, all was silent.

The lights reflected off the carcass of the fallen robot once more, and she had an idea. At least she didn't have to be unarmed. Striding over to where the little fellow lay, she carefully uncovered its body, though specifically it was the arms she was after. It had four, spindly, multi-jointed affairs. Two ended in pincers, but the others led to sockets into which various attachments could be slotted. In one she found a small trowel, in the other a three-pronged fork.

Removing them wasn't easy, because the connections were rusted, but with some effort she yanked both free.

As weapons went, neither was especially lethal, but even so she felt better. Of the two the trowel seemed sharper, so she gingerly stuck the fork into the waistband of her pants, nestled in the small of her back, then peered into the forest.

There were still no other sounds. A gentle breeze wafted over her, carrying with it the scent of flora run amok, a mélange of different odours assailing her nostrils, and she was glad hay fever was something else she didn't suffer from.

She took a few steps into the undergrowth. Though it was thick, the branches and leaves parted like curtains. As she walked deeper in, the foliage she'd passed through closed behind her, and it became gloomier.

Her heart was pounding and her hands trembled. This was ridiculous. Pressing on into the forest when she hadn't any inkling what was going on was stupid. She was by herself with only a couple of gardening implements for protection.

Another cry pierced the air. It sounded near. It sounded like the owner of the voice was in pain.

She thought of rushing forth to find the source, but reconsidered. She'd been reckless enough to go this far, and she ascribed this to the lingering aftereffects of her slumber. Her mind less muzzy now, she knew she needed to head back to the main chamber and start waking people up. Then, when they had safety in numbers, they would return here and sort matters out.

She whirled around, but only took a single step before she paused. Through the brush she could see the transit shaft, into the still open pod, and then she saw something walk in front of the light.

Something big.

Bigger than a man.

Her trembling had become full-blown shakes now. As she watched, the shadowy figure crept into the pod. She saw him—she was pretty sure it was a 'he' even if he was little more than a silhouette—squat down and touch at the floor, and she remembered her bilious vomit.

He stood, lifting his chin as if sniffing the air. Either her eyesight was failing... or else he had horns. Two arms, two legs, though as he turned in profile Imogen vaguely perceived that something wasn't right about his legs.

He exited the transit pod. The doors shut, and a few seconds later Imogen's heart sank as she saw the pod head back towards the ship.

The figure was still sniffing the air. Trying to smell *her*, she realized, and at the same moment she understood what was so off about his silhouette. The legs were jointed the wrong way, the knees facing backwards like a… like a…

She dispelled the thought, concentrated on practicalities. If this thing aimed to hang around here preventing her from calling the transit pod back, then she still had another option. On the other side of the torus was another transit tube, primarily intended for cargo, but it could be used to transport people in an emergency.

She suspected this counted as one.

The trouble was she had to hike through the forest to get to it.

What choice do I have, she thought, besides trying to sneak past that creature?

An alien? The notion wasn't yet embedding itself in her mind. After over a century of humans watching the skies there still has been no evidence of other intelligent life in the universe, which made the pilgrimage to 47 Ursae Majoris more critical. Earth wasn't the ravaged planet at Death's door a lot of fiction writers had predicted, but it was vulnerable nonetheless, and having all your eggs in one basket, even a basket the size of a planet, was a risk.

That was why she and 899 others had volunteered for this project, a one-way trip to the new world. Of course, hostile alien life had been considered, but not as a major prospect.

Always assuming he's hostile, and always assuming he's alien.

Imogen almost laughed, but there was a logical angle to that thought. Vesta and her sister ships could only manage 25% light speed, so the forty-six light year trek would span almost two centuries. Whilst the scientists didn't anticipate any major breakthrough in space travel, there was always the chance that some kind of faster-than-light drive would be invented before their journey was complete. More than once she and her colleagues had joked about waking up to find future humans had gotten to 47 Ursae Majoris before them.

And if space flight technology had advanced, then what progress had genetics might have made? For all she knew the creature over there wasn't alien, but some state-of-the-art hybrid explicitly bred for interstellar travel.

He was moving closer to the edge of the forest now, so she could see him more clearly. He was well over six feet tall, and naked, and those were definitely horns jutting up from his head. His legs were like those of an animal, and between them a large, flaccid penis dangled. His upper body was more human, though his skin was matted with dark hair. He looked strong, powerful.

She felt something stir. She'd been trying to get a better look at his face, but suddenly her gaze was drawn downwards, back to between his legs. My God he's huge, she thought, and not even aroused yet.

She bit her bottom lip. She was still trembling, but it wasn't just fear anymore. It was excitement. An urge was building within her, a desperate yearning to stroll out of the forest and greet him. He was no alien, no danger to her—in fact, if anything she knew he would protect her. He'd wrap those big burly arms around her and draw her close, and then...

He turned away and started striding unnaturally back towards the transit shaft, then veered around it and continued off into the undergrowth on the other side of the clearing.

A wave of disgust washed over her. What the hell was I thinking?, she wondered. Then she realized that the fingers of her left hand had slipped inside the waistband of her pants.

She snatched them out, horrified at her own weakness, her own complicity in the spell that had seemed to overcome her, and that thing...

A man with the legs of a goat!

Like Pan. Imogen tried to remember if Pan was a Roman or Greek figure. It got confusing when your ship and ship's computer were named after the Greek and Roman equivalent of each other.

Whichever, that thing had looked more like something from myth than either an alien or a hybrid; unless Pan had been an extraterrestrial, or human geneticists had thought it amusing to make their creations resemble something from the Elysian Fields.

Whatever he was, now that he had moved on, Imogen was not remotely inclined to trust his motives were pure. She just had to work out what to do now.

Assuming he had really gone, she could go and call the transit pod back, but there would be a wait, and the clearing appeared way too exposed. While she could no longer see him, she had the strangest feeling he hadn't ventured off far.

Maybe he hadn't been able to smell her, but he'd seen her vomit, and likely surmised she might return.

Unless he was right now stalking her from behind.

No, that made no sense. Given the effect he'd had on her whilst still several meters away, he had no reason for subterfuge. If he had waited another few seconds she would've gone to him.

Another cry echoed from the distance.

Imogen shuddered.

Plan B it is, she thought to herself. Circle around the torus and hope she can reach the cargo pod.

That cry though. Despite every instinct telling her not to, she had to investigate, needed to know what they... what *she* was up against. Hell, she had to head in that direction anyway.

She set out cautiously, minimizing the making of any noise. It was a slog, the undergrowth dense. She spied very little fruit on the trees and this puzzled her, as did the absence of any animals. She had spotted none, nor any evidence of them, no tracks, no spoor. She and her sister had hunted enough occasions with her parents for her to recognize signs of wildlife.

The further she probed into the forest, the more anxious she became. Artificial light sprinkled through the branches overhead like raindrops, but it still left the world too dreary for her liking, and the place felt warmer than it should have, and the air, the sickly sweet fragrance that clung to the air...

She had an instant flashback to the fairy tales of her childhood, when dad sat by the bunk bed she and Alicia shared and narrated fables of mystical lands and enchanted forests, where all manner of weird and wonderful (and sometimes frightening) creatures had lived.

Her stomach grumbled. She really wished there was some fruit around here because the nausea had long passed, replaced with hunger.

Another cry, closer now, and abruptly the undergrowth began to thin. She slinked forwards, until she could discern in the distance another clearing.

Something was there.

She crouched just inside the screen of trees and stared out at the tableau before her, unable at first—unwilling—to admit what she was seeing was real.

A naked woman knelt on all fours amidst the shallow grass, and bent over her was one of those creatures. Their hips were driving back and forth in unison as they rutted like beasts.

Imogen felt tears welling in her eyes. She recognized the young Japanese woman. Katsumi Yoshida. She was a botanist who loved to sing and enjoyed watching old 3D movies, and now here she was, being ravished by this…

Satyr! That was what they were called.

A part of her wanted to bolt out and save her colleague from this degradation, but instead Imogen prowled the perimeter of the clearing until she could observe the pair head on. Her eyes widened as she stared at the woman she'd been friends with, a woman who was quiet, unassuming, *innocent*.

Katsumi's face was a twisted mask, and initially Imogen read it as pain that was contorting her features, then realized it was closer to ecstasy. Her teeth were bared in primal lust, eyes shut in reverie, and now Imogen could see that she was thrusting her hips back as forcefully as the satyr was thrusting forwards.

Then another cry echoed out, only from him this time, a high-pitched grunt, and after a moment Katsumi joined him in climax.

They separated, with the satyr dropping back onto the ground, uttering another grunt as he did so, one that sounded all too satisfied.

Katsumi did not run away. She flung herself on top of him, embracing his torso tightly as she kissed him.

Imogen recalled the queer feeling she'd had before when she was near one of these satyrs. She gripped the trowel in her hand tighter. This wasn't the opportunity to intervene. She had to get to the cargo pod, wake the whole damn crew up if necessary.

In the clearing the satyr now sat up, and in his hands was a musical instrument—a flute, not panpipes, Imogen noted. He began to play, a rough, shrill tune, and as he did so Katsumi stood and danced around him. Imogen heard her giggling like a schoolgirl.

She left them to it and moved on. Once again the under-growth grew riotous. At times it was so dark she wondered if night had fallen. But when she looked up she could make out the lights that ran around the inside of the torus' roof high above. That dotted line of illumination was her guide; as long as it was above her she'd reach the other shaft.

She could still hear the satyr's flute as she walked, though it faded with each step. She wondered if Katsumi was still dancing to the satyr's tune, wondered if she had any sense what had happened to her.

Anger threatened to overwhelm her, but Imogen held firm to reason. She eventually noticed the forest dwindling again. Now she heard music coming from ahead of her. The song had that same almost chaotic timbre to it, but it was also obvious it was being produced by more than one instrument. Parts sounded like another flute, but overlapping this were different, hollow sounds.

She slowed down. As well as the music, she thought she heard voices. That sickly sweet smell in the air was more pronounced and hinted of smoke. She thought back to what she had seen earlier when looking up at the torus from the main ship. Someone had lit a fire here.

Something rustled behind her. Imogen turned fast on her heels, eyes wide as she scanned the verdure. She could make out nothing, but she could definitely hear movement, and it was definitely drawing nearer.

She began to gradually retreat, wielding the trowel before her.

The rustling intensified, and now she saw the branches swaying as something approached her. Panicked, fearful of getting too close to one of the satyrs lest she fall under its spell, she quickened her own backward pace and made to turn so she could start running, which was when she was blinded by the sudden brightness, and tumbled as the earth gave way beneath her right foot.

She cursed as she collapsed, letting out a yelp of pain and fright once she realized what she stumbled into. She'd landed on her rump, her right foot planted in a shallow ditch several meters square. The ditch was filled with bleached white bones.

Now I know where the animals went, she thought as she extricated herself. She wondered if this was the only such grave, or if it was just one of many. Her eyes slid over chicken bones, sheep skulls, and… her breath snagged in her throat as her gaze fixed on a single human skull discarded towards the far end of the ditch.

"It really isn't as bad as you think it is."

Imogen wheeled around toward the direction of the voice. When she expelled the breath she'd been holding, it came out as a strangled gasp.

A woman ambled out of the forest. She wasn't naked, but all she wore was a T-shirt that was several sizes too large, so it looked like a ragged dress. Her legs and feet were bare and streaked with dirt.

She was slim, haggard. Her hair was long and unkempt, predominantly grey, though here and there were strands that still retained the same straw-coloured hue as Imogen's. She was smiling, and creases spread across her face like cracks in an old wall.

"Alicia," Imogen whispered.

Her twin sister.

Alicia took a poised step forwards. Instinctively Imogen brandished the trowel, and her sister halted. "You really don't need that," she said. "I know you're confused, but there really is nothing to worry about."

"Nothing to worry about?! I just saw Katsumi Yoshida being raped by a monster, and you…" Tears stung her eyes. "Jesus, sis, how long have you been awake?"

"A long time," answered Alicia, her eyes sparkling. "A long, wondrous time." As she spoke, her hands seemed to move of their own volition, one trailing up towards a breast, the other gently drifting lower…

Now it was Imogen who stepped forwards. "Stop that!" she yelled, caution gone, replaced by fury. "Just stop it."

"As you wish." Her sister raised up her hands in mock surrender. "It's hard to explain to you how wonderful the feeling is, and Katsumi wasn't being raped. She's been awake for over a month now and willingly spends every moment with Ruck."

Imogen blinked her tears away. "Ruck. That's its name?"

"*His* name, sister. They're men. Oh, and such men…"

Imogen was shaking her head. "It's an illusion, whatever you're feeling. Hypnosis, pheromones, or fuck, it may even be magic. I don't care what caused it, it isn't natural."

Alicia nodded. "Oh, I know that, but Parn, beautiful Parn was with me when I woke, and I've been his ever since." She grinned mischievously. Her hands began to rove again. It looked like she was fighting to restrain herself from fondling her own body. "There was a mistake. Parn was supposed to be there when you awoke, but Seff miscalculated the revival time. Set you going, then promptly got drunk and forgot. But it doesn't matter now. You're here, you came here willingly, and together we can go to Parn." She held out her hand.

Imogen's whole body started to quiver. "No."

Alicia cocked her head to one side and smiled sadly. "You don't have a choice, Imo. If you try to flee eventually you'll stray close to one of them, fall under his influence and once you do, you won't ever have to worry anymore. Why delay that bliss? Why be afraid when you can always be happy here in paradise?"

Then a thought struck Imogen. "He's not here, none of them are, so why are you still in its thrall? Why haven't you snapped out of it?"

Another smile. Her sister now resembled their mother, wearing that same patronizing expression she would give whenever one of them said something foolish. "The effect is cumulative. A few hours in their presence is enough, allowing them to shoot their seed inside you a couple of times, and after that…" Alicia closed her eyes and let out a moan.

"Oh my God," said Imogen.

Her sister opened her eyes again. The dreamy eroticism had suddenly vanished. "You won't need god once Parn lays you down. You won't care about 47 Ursae Majoris, or Earth, or anything. All that will matter is being with him."

Imogen shook her head.

Alicia's eyes narrowed. "I promised him you. He adores me, but I've grown old, and he deserves someone young to love as well as me. Who better than my twin sister? Together he will love us, and we him, until death do us part. And. You. Won't. Spoil. That!"

Alicia hurled herself at Imogen.

"Don't!" the younger woman shrieked, reflexively raising the trowel.

Maybe Alicia didn't believe she'd actually do it. Maybe she thought Imogen would lower the weapon.

Or maybe, on some level, buried deep within her, she hoped that Imogen wouldn't.

The metal blade plunged into her body just below the sternum, momentum driving it in all the way to the hilt. There was no cry of pain, no enraged final words, no pitiful last look in her sister's eyes. Alicia uttered a tiny terminal sigh, then fell back onto the grass, eyes staring sightlessly up through the branches to the eternity of space beyond.

Imogen gaped at the dead body of her sister, eyes focused on the trowel sunk in her chest, then on the blood that now stained her own hands. She was in shock, paralyzed for several moments. Then she folded to her knees and wept. She wanted to scream, wanted to loose a searing howl of anger and guilt. She suppressed it because she still heard faint music in the distance.

She forced herself to stand, forced herself to wrench her gaze away from the corpse of a sister she barely recognized anymore. She made herself stagger onwards. Her only hope was to make it to the cargo pod.

She skirted the open grave, trying to disregard the human skull within, not speculating who else had spent decades in "bliss" before dying and being laid to rest here. She thought about the dozen or so empty suspension pods in the main ship. Dear God how long had they been here?

The forest resumed again, but here it was sparser, and as she pressed on she quickly realized her plan of getting to the second shaft wasn't going to be possible. The vegetation was definitely thinning, and pretty soon it wouldn't provide much cover. Then she drew close to another, larger clearing, and as she crouched at the edge she knew with certainty that she couldn't proceed.

This was where the music originated from, a vast exposed area dominated by a huge bonfire, with several smaller campfires scattered around it. The fires, as well as pots and lean-tos, indicated this was where they lived.

And they were there too, the satyrs and their concubines. Three of the creatures. One of them was shambling around the main fire, as if dancing. His demeanour suggested he was drunk. He held a tankard in each hand and as he danced liquid sloshed over the rims. Every few seconds he'd pause to take a gulp from one or the other.

The other two satyrs were propped up against tree stumps. Each was playing an instrument, one a flute, the other honest-to-God panpipes. A naked woman attended to each as they performed, pleasuring them with their mouths in their own perverted parody of musicality.

It was no longer disturbing to Imogen—though it helped that she couldn't identify the women from this vantage, nor the third who was curled up asleep near one of the smaller fires—but as her gaze trailed back towards the drunken creature by the large fire, she finally noted something that did shock her, that drove her even closer to the brink of insanity.

A wooden frame had been erected around the fire, and a spit ran through it. Impaled on the spit was a charred hunk of cooked flesh. It had no legs and no head, but a very human arm hung limply into the flames. She wasn't certain, but there seemed enough detail to guess that it had once belonged to a man.

Of course, she thought as she considered the ghastly logic of the situation. What other use would the satyrs have for men? After they had consumed all the animals and fermented most of the fruit, what else were they going to eat?

She silently wept for Alicia, for Katsumi, and the other women here, and for the nameless man on the spit—she prayed to God he'd been dead before they'd cooked him.

The drunken satyr stopped dancing, chugged the contents of one tankard and threw it away with a loud burp. He then proceeded to rip the arm from the grilling corpse like it was a chicken wing, and that was when Imogen snapped.

She bit her lip to stifle the scream that was mounting, but that was the limit of her restraint. She spun around and sprinted back the way she'd come. She was scratched and grazed by the undergrowth as she hurried through it. But she didn't care about pain, didn't care about keeping quiet. All that mattered was getting away from that horrifying campsite.

She slowed down only once, when she reached the pit of bones, and only enough to allow her to circumnavigate it with care before she increased her speed once more. She did not dare look for Alicia's body, knowing well that if she saw her again shock would set in and Imogen would shut down and collapse, scrunch herself up into a ball until some goat-legged bastard showed up to make her his bitch.

She veered slightly to the left in hopes of missing Katsumi and her satyr, and kept glancing up every so often to ensure she was still following the lights back towards the main transit shaft.

And all the while she expected some monster to lurch out of the undergrowth and seize her.

Frantic, she burst out of the forest into the tangle around the transit shaft. Only when she had rushed up to the metal cylinder and slapped the call button, only when her gasps for air eased into more normal breaths as she waited, only then did she remember why she'd been heading for the cargo pod in the first place.

Imogen turned, but it was too late.

He was standing right behind her, scarcely a yard away, like some giant from a storybook. Terror barely had time to sink its claws into her before the emotion faded like mist, and new, alien feelings took hold.

An elongated shiver seemed to caress her whole body, every part of her flesh prickling in anticipation as she stared at him. Her legs almost buckled, and she had to lean back against the closed doors of the transit tube to keep herself upright.

He was huge, bigger than any of the others, his shoulders broad, his chest rippled with muscle, ringlets of dark hair coating his naked body. His jaw was square, his face angular as if it'd been chiseled from rock, and the horns that rose up from his head were long and thick.

But it was his eyes, the penetrating gaze of those blue lasers that drove her wild. And this close she could smell him, a pungent, bestial musk. The headiest aroma she had ever encountered.

"I am Parn," he said, his voice smooth, strong, masterful. She already loved it. "You are Imogen, and you are mine."

Another shiver took hold of her as he said those words, because she wanted to be his, to adore and worship him as her sister had.

And then the doors to the transit tube opened and she tumbled backwards, her hands stretching forlornly out to grab him, but he was just a little too far away.

Whether it was the sight of her sister's blood on her hands, the jolt of pain as she hit the floor and the fork in her waistband dug into her spine, or a combination of the two, she didn't know, but suddenly the spell was broken and she was in control once more.

Parn didn't realize this as he reached down with a meaty hand to help her up, a lascivious smile on his face that would have telegraphed his intentions even if the member between his legs wasn't already making them abundantly clear.

The scent that had intoxicated her just moments before now repulsed her. He smelt sickly, unclean, but she reached up with her left hand and took his anyway.

As he hoisted her to her feet, her right hand gripped the garden fork behind her. As soon as she was standing, terrified that the hypnotic miasma would return, she struck, jabbing the fork towards the exposed gap beneath his left arm.

He yowled as the tines punctured flesh. She tugged the weapon free and struck once more, thrusting it towards his stomach now. A crashing flashback of doing the same to Alicia enraged her—she was angry at herself as much as him—but she took it all out on Parn, withdrawing the tines and stabbing him yet again.

Parn swung his right arm in a wide arc, intending to knock her head off with his massive fist, but he was big and unwieldy, not to mention wounded, so she had time to extract the fork and duck under his arm before ramming the weapon into his side, hoping there was a kidney there.

Parn roared with pain. With an unexpected, ferocious surge of energy he jerked away. The fork was wrenched from Imogen's hand, and as he staggered back it stayed firmly planted in his flank.

She was defenseless now, and her mind raced to come up with something she could improvise as a weapon. The robot's remaining arms might be useful, but the satyr was between her and the droid.

Parn stared at her. There was a look in his eyes beyond anger, yet also tinged with surprise. Perhaps no woman had ever resisted before. Who knew how old he was, how many women he'd used and discarded.

He gazed down, almost uncomprehendingly, at the fork protruding from his side. Then he yanked it out. He studied the tines dripping with his blood, then directed his attention back at Imogen.

She raised her chin defiantly and clenched her hands into tiny fists, knowing they'd be ineffectual against him, but knowing she'd fight to the last anyway.

He dropped the fork, then crumpled to his knees. For a moment he just knelt there, head bowed as if in prayer. Then Imogen jumped when he threw his head back and let out a long, thunderous bellow. It cut through her like a knife, and she imagined it would be heard throughout the torus.

And then it was over, and Parn slumped to the ground. She watched him for several seconds, but he didn't move again, didn't utter another sound.

It could be a trick, she supposed, but she couldn't waste time worrying. That bellow had not just been a death rattle, it'd been a summons. The others would be coming.

She looked behind her into the transit pod. She could get in and be back on the ship in seconds. But they'd follow. It would take time to wake anyone else, time she wouldn't have. No, she had to neutralize the threat before she left.

The computer was still active. She accessed the environmental controls. It proved almost pathetically easy to adjust the atmospheric settings. If Hestia had still been online she wouldn't have been able to do what she was attempting, but in dumb-mode far too many safety protocols were disabled.

With the job done she dashed toward the pod, just as several figures barrelled from the forest. I'm not going to make it, she thought, but then the group halted by Parn's corpse, and their pause gave her valuable moments to get inside and into a harness.

Satyrs and women, Katsumi among them, stared down at Parn's body. Then they eyed Imogen with a murderous rage that showed no distinction between human and satyr, and she knew she'd had no choice but to do what she'd done. These women were no longer the people they'd been. They were hostage to the satyrs' lust, and probably always would be.

With a scream made up of many voices they charged at her.

Imogen had already pushed the launch button, but the doors didn't shut until a heartbeat before they reached the pod. There was a thump as something impacted the closed doors, and she watched as the metal began to bend inwards.

Then she was gone, hurtling upwards. The turbulence was not so bad this time, and the clanking as the pod passed from one tube to the next was no longer unsettling, but reassuring.

She hadn't been sure she would make it in time, but then the pod slowed and came to a halt. She was upside down, but there was no gravity here so this wasn't a problem. She unbuckled the harness and floated out of the pod and into the service corridor.

She peered up at the forest rotating overhead. It looked no different.

Did I miscalculate, she thought, why isn't it—

And then a tsunami of fire tore around the torus, a sea of flames that would incinerate every tree and satyr and woman within. For a handful of seconds the endless night was lit up by the blazing forest that had become a giant Catherine wheel in space. Imogen had to shield her eyes from the glare.

She'd ramped up the oxygen levels within the torus way past their safety margins, and also vented hydrogen in from the tertiary fuel reserves. After that, all that had been needed was a spark. The satyrs' own campfires had ignited the very air itself.

The inferno above her head died as instantaneously as it had begun. Probably the explosive conflagration had cracked the hull of the torus; vacuum had fought fire and won.

Imogen knew there was no way anything inside could've survived. She sank to the cold floor and continued to stare up at the dark, ruined wheel, still turning. Soon she would have to start waking people, but right now she just wanted to rest, and shed tears for her sister and the others. There was now a tender empty hole inside of her that she feared might never be refilled.

And then a delicate voice echoed through her mind, the comforting algorithmic song of Hestia as she came back on-line. Imogen shook her head.

"Where were you when I needed you?" she asked, but got no reply. Hestia it seemed had other things on her mind, a ship adrift in space and the destruction of Section Zero to name but two.

Maybe the satyrs affected Hestia in some way, Imogen mused. Or maybe, she countered herself, it's true what they say, that even goddesses only help those who help themselves.

An Amuse Bouche

Lizz-Ayn Shaarawi

"They really are quite a treat, once you get past the way they stare at you," Anton assured Livie as he escorted her to the table. With a shudder of both delight and revulsion, Livie took her seat at the large table in the center of the room. Next to her sat a hulking figure, its green and purple skin freckled with shiny flat spots.

Though they insisted they had come in peace, it was still taking most humans a while to become completely comfortable around the Zarlians. To assuage fears, the new visitors gave the people of Earth technological, agricultural, and medical advances that had literally overnight erased famine, poverty, and disease. But everybody knows you don't get something for nothing and Livie made sure to keep one eye on the alien to her right.

The table soon filled with the who's who of Earth, intermixed with the Zarlian diplomatic assembly. Rock stars, actors, billionaires, and politicians rubbed elbows with their alien equivalents as wine was poured and conversation politely drifted through the room. Then the aliens stopped speaking and turned en mass towards a door at the far corner of the room, causing the humans to bristle. Panicked looks shot between people as the door flew open, but relaxed once they realized what drew the creatures' attention.

Kilted waiters carried tray upon tray of appetizers, some recognizable to the humans, others clearly alien. Delicate aromas filled the air, causing more than one guest's stomach to rumble. The aliens' bellies gurgled visibly, the skin shifting as their abdomens undulated. Livie tried not to stare, but it was difficult not to notice the expansive torso—it wasn't as if the aliens were small by any stretch of the imagination. They were eight feet tall with broad shoulders that expanded down to rounded pouches, stopping at long, tree trunk-like legs, capped with flat, wide feet. Their faces were the worst part. Part fish, part gorilla, bulging eyes sat on either side of high, sloping foreheads that rounded down past upturned noses and wide, thick-lipped mouths on protruding jaws.

Livie turned away from the spectacle of the alien's belly and downed the rest of her wine in one gulp. Thankfully, a waiter immediately refilled her glass.

Platters were placed at intervals along the table. The guests passed their plates around and were rewarded with canapés and shrimp puffs, as well as white tubers flecked with a pink lacey garnish and multicolored discs drenched in a variety of toppings.

Livie held a lavender disc up to her nose and sniffed. She wasn't sure what she was expecting, but the sensual tropical scent that filled her nostrils wasn't it. Her eyes widening in surprise, she gave a small nibble, only to find her mouth flooded with the taste of pineapple combined with cherry. The topping, pearly rose beads, popped in her mouth with a slight salty-sweet flavor. It wasn't until she nipped her own fingers that she realized she had eaten the rest of the disc. A quick glance around the room proved that she wasn't the only human enjoying the new delicacies. Eyes closed, the other humans practically groaned in ecstasy as they devoured the appetizers, some licking their fingers clean. The aliens, though dining from the trays as well, appeared to enjoy watching the humans eat even more than the food itself.

Anton gently kicked Livie under the table and mouthed the words "just wait." At that exact moment, the waiters returned, this time swapping the empty plates for finger bowls. After the places were cleared, the waiters bustled out again, leaving the guests to make uneasy conversation, though not for long.

Once more, the doors at the far end of the room swung open. The waiters returned, each carrying a small plate on which rested a single soupspoon. A plate was set in front of each guest. A few of the diners shrieked when they glanced down. Curled in each spoon was a small, slug-like creature. The shrieks were the result of seeing the creature not only still alive, but actively watching the diners in return.

Anton stood and raised his glass. "Our generous guests, the Zarlians, have provided an *amuse bouche*—a little treat for the mouth—for us tonight." The Zarlians' lips pulled back into what Livie assumed was supposed to be a smile but, with their triangular razor sharp teeth gleaming in the candlelight, was more threatening than reassuring.

Anton continued, "Commander Snar, if you would."

The Zarlian beside Livie stood and held an oval piece of metal to his throat. When he spoke, his mouth moved to form words in Zarli, though the oval broadcast the words in English.

"Thank you, Mr. Anton, for your generous hospitality. I do hope dinners such as these can further the understanding between our two worlds."

Snar picked up the spoon, showing the contents to the table. The contents stared right back.

"We present to you a Lobnot. It is a creature known for its excellent flavor, as well as a faint euphoric effect when ingested. If cooked, the creature not only loses the euphoric quality but also develops a bitter, tough taste. So it is best to swallow it raw, like one of your oysters. We hope you enjoy these more exotic tastes of Zarl here on Earth."

Most of the humans waited until the Zarlians slurped their Lobnots down before placing it to their lips. Anton gulped his down immediately.

"Delicious! Go on, Livie. You'll love it. Trust me."

A few of the other humans had choked theirs down as well. Livie watched as they slumped in their seats, eyelids drooping, and crooked smiles played on their lips.

"Go on," Anton slurred.

Snar peered down at her with his great bulging eyes. "Yes, go on." He held the spoon to her mouth. Her lips parted and the Lobnot darted off the spoon, skittered across her tongue, and forced its way down her throat. She tried to gag but the creature was already down her esophagus.

It only took moments for the onset of the effects. Livie felt her mouth water and her skin tingle. Heat radiated out from her belly to her extremities. A feeling of complete calm washed over her.

"There, isn't that better now?" Snar asked, his piranha grin glinting.

Livie swiveled in her seat at the sound of his voice. Her eyes focused on the green and purple skin, the shiny flecks that stippled across it. Mouth drooling, belly burning, she lunged forward and bit a chunk out of Snar's neck. Warm blue blood ran down her chin as she chewed slowly, savoring the meaty flavor that spread over her taste buds, even as his screams filled her ears.

Some of the humans recoiled in horror. Others smiled and turned on the remaining Zarlians. A female Zarlian broke from the table and lumbered towards the door, but two humans tackled her, ripping her apart before her body hit the floor. Blue splatters decorated the walls. Hoarse bellows were cut short by snapping jaws and grinding teeth.

Livie sat, legs splayed beneath her expensive designer gown, and snapped Snar's femur to suck the marrow from it. Anton, gnawing on a hand, slid down to the floor beside her. She grinned at him, her teeth coated in blue film.

"You're right," she said. "They really are quite the treat once you get past them staring at you."

Halo

Ben Pienaar

Several weeks had passed since he committed suicide before David went into his father's office. The body had been harvested just a few days afterward, but until now, on the second Sunday of the New Year, he'd been too busy. Only a distant, nagging curiosity prompted him to enter the dusty room, and once he was inside, he wasn't entirely sure what he wanted to do.

His father had gone the way most everyone did when they disabled their halos. First they grew depressed, then fell into a deep sleep, and upon waking were irreversibly insane. Most just killed themselves, but a few went on full-blown rampages, murdering everyone they encountered until the law took them down. His father had hanged himself.

David had often thought idly about disabling his own halo, but he couldn't quite understand people who went ahead and did it.

Then again, he found himself tempted to try it, just to see what all the fuss was about. Surely, if he prepared himself mentally beforehand, he would be able to resist whatever mad impulse had caused his father to kill himself.

And if not... well, at least then he would know. That was something, wasn't it?

But David had not disabled his halo. It remained atop his head, a luminous circle on a wire protruding from his skull like an antenna—which was, he knew, one of the many functions it had.

He walked over to his father's desk and sat down in front of it. It was covered with piles of old tax forms and banking documents (his father had been an accountant), as well as torn pieces of newspaper articles.

Most, but not all of these, had the word 'halo' in their headlines.

The second Sunday of the New Year was, incidentally, the day celebrating the invention of the first halo, and that made it the only official holiday of the year and the only day in which no one really got anything done. Most people just lay around and basked in the glow of their implants, or slept for the whole day.

David felt anxious, the halo's response to inactivity, and he spent a few minutes staring at the wall and contemplating sleep. But then, there was that curiosity, and eventually he gathered himself and started to read.

He began with the oldest article first, meaning to proceed in chronological order. It was from a journal dated Sunday, 13th January, 2013. It was so dry and yellowed he suspected it would crumble to dust if he held it too tightly.

First Permanent Behaviour Modifier
Experiment Success

This week, world-renowned ethologist Dr. Garth C. Dennis published a report of his recent success in the specialised field of behaviour modification. The doctor has dubbed his invention the 'halo', and admits that while it is still in the developmental stages, he has seen great potential in its application on chimpanzees. From a worryingly large number of chimps rescued from the wild, Dennis selected ten of the most aggressive males and confined them for several weeks, five each to an enclosure. Predictable violence ensued—e.g., posturing, teeth baring, screeching— in the enclosure with the non-implanted chimps. In the other, the halo-grafted chimps strolled, lounged, and often slept, and no competition, fighting, or any conflict occurred. In fact, these chimps were only casually interested in their food, and no stealing or protective behaviour was observed.

For the animal welfare conscious, Dennis assures that the halo device connected to the neural pathways in the chimps was not any kind of negative reinforcement. 'I do not believe in the stick,' he says, invoking a classical analogy, 'but the carrot.' The halo is designed to raise dopamine levels and lower cortisol levels, which Dennis claims leaves the subject feeling happy, tranquil, and satisfied at all times.

Not a bad way to live, it would seem, but the device is still in its early trials. 'With the halo, there is no desire to do anything, unfortunately,' Dennis admits. 'In humans, this would be disastrous for society. I'm also concerned that in the long term the chimps would be content to starve or walk off a cliff. There is a chance their fear instincts may be inhibited.'

Despite its drawbacks, Dennis is not short on funding and has high hopes for the future of the halo.

'I dream of perfecting a device that will replace the darker side of human nature with only good,' he said. 'In my ideal world, there will be no pain, fear, or violence. I really believe this can happen.'

David yawned and riffled through a few more of the papers. There were several dated within the same time frame but he decided to skip forward much further. The topic was already boring him. What he really wanted to do was go to his room and study for a few hours, maybe even skip sleep for the night. What a rush! But he was still curious—slightly— and the next article promised to be more interesting. Glued to the top of the page was a clipping from a flyer: *'Halo Perfected for Human Testing, Volunteers Wanted!'* along with a brief description of the desired subjects and expected effects. Beneath this, the article read:

20th June 2019
First Halos® Released for Sale

Barely a year ago, acclaimed researcher Dr. Garth C. Dennis announced that his Halo® machine was now perfected and ready for human trials. Since then, the device has been tested on more than three hundred individuals and as yet not a single one has given a negative review. In fact, when their machines were disabled, many commented that they felt mildly depressed afterwards and missed the 'warm glow' and 'exhilaration' of the Halo®. In the post-test surveys, all participants agreed that they would purchase the device without a moment's hesitation, some even going so far as to say that cost would not be an issue.

Hospitals all across the country will begin offering a Halo® installation from the 18th November at a bargain price of two thousand US dollars ($2,000.00). While much cheaper than a car and not much more expensive than a television, Dennis has commented that he regrets the "high fee" the hospitals have insisted upon, saying that such a revolutionary innovation should be available to people of all economic strata.

The installation can be performed at any certified hospital with an appropriately licensed surgeon, and even though it is brain surgery, there is no need to worry. The risks are minor, and only a local anaesthetic is required. For those wary of malfunctioning devices, the Halo® can be easily disabled with no more than a screwdriver and a steady hand.

David wondered what it had been like in a world without halos. He knew in theory—they studied it in History class—but still, he wondered. He'd had his installed on his third birthday, but it wasn't like he could remember that long ago. All he'd ever known was the halo, and that was fine by him. He *felt* fine.

From what he had learned, the emotions of 'sadness' and 'terror' were not something anyone would want, but now David asked himself, how did anyone really *know* that? Well, his father had known. He'd only had his halo installed when he was twenty-five, but then he'd disabled his nevertheless, so what did *that* tell you?

He hanged himself, an inner voice whispered.

Another voice replied, *but still…*

David shook his head to clear it, and experienced a fresh wash of pleasantness, like warm sunshine through an open window. He was used to these, but they still felt so good. Maybe taking off the halo was a bad idea if it meant never getting a rush anymore. He decided to keep reading. Mental activity tended to excite it.

He picked up the next article.

Halo 3.0 and new Halo programmes
available for purchase

13th January, 2020. Today is the sixth anniversary of Dr. Dennis's invention of the first Halo prototype in 2013, and he is proud to announce his latest model 3.0, as well as a number of new supplementary programmes. Fitness 1 ™, an easily installed addition, is compatible with Halo models 2.0 and 3.0 and produces a surge of natural euphorias during aerobic and muscular exercise, with an automatic cut-off when the body is overtaxed. There is also HaloTaste ™ which alters tastebud perception, causing the user to taste healthy foods such as vegetables and grains as delicious treats and unhealthy foods as repulsive in flavour. For other programme information, consult your local Halo store.

David flipped the paper over but there was nothing else written on it. He rifled through the contents of the desk until he came upon a more recent scrap. There was a date scrawled in his father's rushed penmanship: *21st May, 2031.* The writing in this article was different, and David presumed its author was himself under the influence of a halo. That was good. David had always had trouble deciphering texts from pre-2021, when no one had halos and couldn't seem to stop describing stuff, especially those endlessly confusing things called feelings. Words were just a way of getting facts into the brain, as far as David was concerned.

President Dennis has recently been nominated for the long overdue Nobel Peace Prize. Since the development of the Halo (and the 'Dennis Act' of 2026, making the Halo a mandatory fixture for all civilians), crime has become an exclusively Third World problem. Throughout most of Europe, Asia, and North America the ratio of police officers to people has dropped to one for every 100,000. Primary causes of death are now disease and accidents, the latter of which serves to feed almost the entire population.

David's own halo was set to begin the mild shocks that very week, reminding him to visit the city for that month's refill. Perhaps his father would be mixed up somewhere in the next capsule of black goo. David's hand drifted to the back of his neck where the current tube was still attached, recycling thousands of the expired into his veins.

With the police force and hospitals decommissioned, and farming replaced with recycling plants, the human race has made leaping technological and, more importantly, political advancements. Only with President Dennis's device has the western world been able to thrive under Communism. For now, President Dennis insists that the West's primary concern should be to manufacture and supply the developing countries with Halos. 'With the world united under one man, one mind so determined as mine—not just for world peace, but universal peace—there are no limits to what human beings may achieve.'

David sometimes found himself questioning whether the halo the President wore was the same as everyone else's. Well, no one's halo was exactly the same as anyone else's, but what kind of programmes did he have in his?

David sighed and gazed out the window, where all the roads and alleys stretched out into a grid. Look toward any point on the compass and it was like peering down an endless corridor lined with identical little white houses. So peaceful.

He got up from the desk and thoughtfully stared for a while at the light fixture. His father had hanged himself from there, and it had been three days before the collectors came for his body. It had started to rot by then, but luckily the halo did not allow him to smell bad things. Not that he would recognize a bad smell, he thought. He could not even comprehend *dis*liking a smell. What could possibly cause a person to block their nose from the world, or for that matter close their eyes, like they did in all the old books?

He stood there motionless and contemplated. He wasn't usually able to do that for long, but the halo was still feeding him some mild endorphins from the reading. These would soon run out, though, and then if he kept standing there doing nothing it would trigger either the morphine or the adrenaline to get him to do something, to get some work done. What happened if you didn't have the halo? Could you just stand and think for as long as you wanted? Would you be overrun with 'bad feelings'? He didn't know.

David found the green-handled screwdriver his father had used to disable his own halo in the top desk drawer. It was not that uncommon for people to disable. Some just got curious, and others did it because they were old enough to remember not having one and wanted to experience it again. Whatever the reason, disabling your own halo almost always resulted in suicide or murder. That wasn't so bad, David thought. If he killed himself he would just get recycled, so it wouldn't be a waste. What did he have to lose?

The halo was beginning to raise his adrenaline now. That was the worst thing about having a holiday, the halo all ready to go and no work to do. Ultimately everyone just ended up cleaning things.

David located the place where the halo wire snaked into his scalp, penetrating his skull. It wasn't the way the original halos had been constructed—those ones had actual screws to undo—however it could still be disabled without too much trouble. Sometimes when they malfunctioned and somebody began destroying public property, a technician would temporarily deactivate their halo and put them to sleep while it got fixed.

He could always call an HT if there was a problem, he reassured himself. Besides that, he was sure it was possible to reattach the halo yourself if you were careful and got all the wires into the hole.

When the tip of the screwdriver hit bone, David felt the halo inject him with something to compensate. He forgot the name of the chemical, but it felt good, until the anaesthetic kicked in and the area went numb. When the warm blood began to leak down the back of his neck, that felt good too.

He dug around until he felt the screwdriver come into contact with the base of the halo, where the wires entered the tiny hole into his skull. David knew that the wire covering stopped a fraction before the skull and that was where he wedged the screwdriver. He got a good grip on it and then pushed, hard.

He heard a loud snap, this followed by a strange buzzing sensation that spread all over his body, and the top part of the halo came off completely and landed on the carpet.

For several seconds his whole body continued to buzz. He couldn't compare such a feeling to anything, because he'd never felt anything truly unpleasant before, but he supposed his father might have likened it to knocking your funny bone (which he said wasn't funny at all), only all over.

When this began to fade, David felt pain for the first time in his life.

It was beyond anything he could have imagined, and still he did not experience all of it. Before the awful burning could extend further than his scalp, he passed out.

When he woke, the pain was still there, and for several minutes he simply lay on the floor, experiencing it. It was unpleasant, that was certain. It was horrible, indescribable, but at the same time he couldn't help savouring it. None of his friends had felt this—only him and the few other daredevils who had disabled their halos.

This was unexplored territory.

But with that thought, the others came, and these he did not savour.

He clenched his eyes shut and tried not to think. He had a monstrous headache and his mouth was dry, but his mind was much too clear. He was beginning to see the truth... no, to *feel* the truth, and that, like the pain, was unpleasant.

Terrified, he rose from the floor and staggered over to the window. He had not been unconscious for long, but the sky was turning orange and darkening already. He had never thought to look at the sky before, and there was a moment of bliss as he comprehended the beauty of the sunset. It did not compare to the halo in the slightest, and it didn't last long.

David was now seeing the rows of little white houses for what they really were: prison cells. A great hive, full of dazed and docile worker bees. He was seeing millions of corpses, collected and processed to feed the living. And he was seeing vast armies of fearless, blank-minded soldiers marching over foreign lands, transforming the inhabitants, sticking halos into their heads and making them into good citizens, or more good soldiers.

David saw all of this, and then he began to cry—also for the first time in his life—because he remembered his father had died only weeks ago, in this very room. When he had heard the news, he'd been vaguely surprised, and then had resumed his homework. He remembered that, too, and for a moment he teetered on the brink. He wanted to kill every man, woman, and child he could find. Not for revenge or hate, but to *save* them.

But he remained still and realised that if anyone had to die, it would be him. He was very tempted. The screwdriver was right there, after all, and no one would mind in the least. He dropped to his knees and stared at it. He imagined his mother coming into the room and discovering him sprawled against the wall in a pool of blood, his jugular punctured. Her brow furrowing in faint puzzlement, perhaps a little curiosity. And then she would calmly go notify the collectors.

David reached for the screwdriver, hesitated, breathing in thick, ragged gasps. His heart thudded in his chest.

This, he thought, was everything they talked about in the books. The madness, the terror, the rage, the pain. He knew it all now.

David moved his hand away from the screwdriver and instead grasped the halo. The base looked slightly bent. *If it doesn't go in*, he thought, *I'll pick up the screwdriver.*

When he reinserted the delicate-looking rod into his scalp and forced the wires back into the tiny hole in his skull, he felt something—a magnet probably—pull them properly inside. The halo clicked neatly into place.

An eternity later, the waves returned. Glorious waves of joy, serenity, and precious endorphins to alleviate his pain.

David exhaled a long sigh of relief, his heartbeat slowed, and he smiled.

It had been close, but then again, many had failed where he had succeeded. He was, in fact, quite proud of himself. He could even show his friends the wound, and they'd have to believe him. He'd be the talk of the school now. He wondered how he was going to describe all the things he'd thought and felt, and realised it would be impossible. He remembered his thoughts, but they made no sense to him now. It was all just so much gibberish.

He looked out the window again, marvelling at how such a spectacular sight could have struck him as horrifying only minutes ago. He rubbed the back of his head absently, then turned and left the office, only pausing for a moment to cast a final glance toward the small, green-handled screwdriver on the desk.

Green

Vince Liberato

My first memories were the dreams I had before I was born. Through these dreams I learned about the world that I would emerge to. It was grey and uniform, perfected over centuries of progress into a machine as efficient as any that ran in the factories that covered the land. I was to be a small part of this machine, as useful as I was replaceable, in a role for which those in my model had been engineered long before I had been authorized for creation.

But the world I awoke to was not the one I had been designed for. The Reset—a global cataclysm that reverted our planet to a primitive and primordial state—occurred hours before my pod opened. In a single day, the whole planet had changed itself back to the way it had been before my fore-bears began modifying their bodies to live in the new world their progress was creating. Within hours, trees and grasses long thought extinct sprouted up from the ground to full maturity, blanketing the planet in suffocating oxygen and everywhere everything became an uncontrolled green.

Only two factories survived The Reset. One of these, the carbolyte plant, is where I live. Its purpose is the creation of carbolyte, a solution designed to feed those that inhabit the plants, my genetically identical worker models. It had been decided long before The Reset that natural reproduction was a chaotic and unfair method of producing workers. In the old world, when one unit either perished through accident or aged past usefulness, it would be replaced—cloned—without a loss of productivity.

Ever since then, not a single living creature created was subjected to the tyranny of genetics. The quantity of perfect workers required was calculated to fulfill the collective needs and were produced to do so, ensuring that all that had been given life had also been given purpose.

The other factory, the air plant, refills biosuit canisters with the atmosphere needed for our existence. Without it, we would choke on the abundance of oxygen and lack of carbon dioxide. Had one of the genetic adjustment labs remained, it would be possible to alter our biology so it would be better adapted to The Reset world, rendering their air production plant useless. For the sake of survival, the two factories have forged the trading agreement: our carbolyte for their air.

As one of the traders, my job is to oversee this exchange.

In the clearing, along the established Tradelines, I could see my barter counterpart waiting for me. I waved my yellow-gloved hand at him from the hill and he returned the gesture with his blue one.

"Hello Blue," I said, using the name we call those from the air plant.

"Hello Yellow," he returned, calling me the name given to us by the Blues.

We moved our two carts to the Tradelines etched into the ground. This spot was chosen because it was the middle point between our factories. It was one of the only places we knew of where no grass grew, and the trees kept the worst of the sun's rays off of us. Our biosuits were fabricated for us to wear inside factories, once considered hazardous areas. Now, ironically, the outside world would kill us much quicker than the factory could, making our suits as essential as carbolyte and air.

"Today I bring you empty tanks and carbolyte to trade," I said to the Yellow. "The tanks are what I will trade for first, at the designated exchange rate of three empty to one full. Do you agree?"

"I agree," the Yellow said. "How many empty tanks did you bring for me?"

"I have ninety-nine tanks for you," I said, pushing my cart forward.

"Thirty-three full tanks for all your empty tanks."

Despite not having a way of producing the air needed to breathe, we Yellows held an advantage when bartering because our product came in dissolvable containers produced by our machines. The Blues required the tanks from us to refill, otherwise they could not move their product. We had amassed enough filled spare tanks for most of us to live off of, in the event trade between our two camps ceased, and we traded only enough food to keep them alive and maintain our advantage. If a trade freeze did occur, we would live longer and could take their plant when they were all dead. We would lose a few of our own Blues to suffocation, but this was deemed acceptable.

"I will give you two carbolyte servings for one air tank," I said, tapping my cart. There were one hundred and thirty-two white tubes left.

"It is supposed to be three," the Blue said. "Why has the number changed?"

"There is trouble at the factory. Some Yellows are now reduced to rationing. You must understand," I said.

"I do understand... I understand that you are cheating me," the Blue replied with the expected answer.

"You must accept. You do not have any other sources of food. I..."

The Blue interrupted me. This was not predictable, as it was not normal behavior. "But we do. Carbolyte from your factory is no longer the only thing we can consume."

"Consume?" I asked. "You are bluffing, Blue." Lying was customary while trading, provided they were credible statements. I was lying about my factory's limits, but my lie was plausible. His was not.

"Perhaps I am, perhaps I am not. I suggest you either trade me your wares at the three-to-one ratio or go back to your factory with the tanks I have already traded to you. I will not need your carbolyte."

"You are not serious." I was more confounded than anything. I tried to think of an explanation for his actions. There was simply no way the Blue could go back without food. If he was not bluffing then—no, he had to be bluffing. There was nothing left after The Reset except crumbling factories and clones.

"I am very serious," the Blue said. "The Yellows will be at the Tradelines again in three days. The exchange rate for tanks remains the same, but carbolyte will be traded at a four-to-one ratio or we will not trade at all."

"Four-to-one!?" I yelled through my mask, temporarily allowing my emotions to take control. This was not normal behavior and my voice surprised me, but I did not restrain myself. "To get that we would have to ration ourselves even further!"

"So be it. I am done here." The Blue turned his back to me and waved his blue, rubber-coated hand. "I will see you in three days."

I waited, convinced that the Blue would at any moment admit defeat and begin the trade as usual. To my shock, he walked away without saying another word. I struggled for an answer. The Blues and the Yellows were supposed to be identical, yet he was doing something that I did not, could not, predict. Irregular behavior did happen on occasion and even emotion sometimes could be manifested, but to turn your back and leave during a trade? He had to be telling the truth. The Blues had found a way to feed themselves.

I took one of the air tanks and crossed over the Trade-lines, stalking the Blue silently.

He whirled around with only enough time to understand what I was going to do. I thrust the tank into his abdomen and he doubled over. I lifted the tank and brought it down on his head several times. He twitched for a minute or so, then stopped moving.

I had to rest following the murder. When I was done, I peeled off the Blue's suit. The helmet was the first thing I removed. The Blue looked like a distorted, bloodied mirror image of myself. More than half his face had been caved in. His eyes were still intact. They gazed into mine through my visor, condemning me.

"It is for our survival," I growled.

He continued to stare.

"And you should have accepted my offer," I added and stripped off my biosuit.

The outside environment would take at least an hour to do significant damage to me, but even so I dressed quickly. The Blue's suit fit exactly as my yellow biosuit did. I put the Blue's body inside of my cart and pushed it off the road into a ditch in Yellow territory. I filled his cart with my carbolyte. It would be a while before any of my comrades realized I was missing. By that time I would have destroyed the Blue food machine, if it really existed. Their survival, and by extension my own, depended on it.

The air factory, like the carbolyte plant, was carved into the side of a mountain above the tree line but below the cold mountaintop. Both structures were roughly the same height above ground, which was why they had been spared destruction from The Reset. From the outside, I could see the Blue's factory was identical to my own and would probably have a similar layout.

At the front gate two Blues were standing guard, with an additional three behind them at the entrance to the building. Several pipes protruded above the third floor. Before The

Reset, they were a polished silver color. Now, they were rusted the very same color as the blood of the Blue I killed smeared inside the stolen biosuit. The exterior brick was deteriorating, with green veins of ivy clinging to the wall, strangling the last bits of the old world to death.

One of the Blues posted at the front gate waved me in. I returned the gesture and pushed the cart over to where a handful of others rested. Several Blues immediately went to empty my cart without giving me a second glance, proving my assumption that Blue and Yellow protocol were identical.

The inside was also near identical to my home. On the third floor I could see the steel walkway that led to the sleep pods. The ground pulsed and shuddered from the operations of the machines below. The main floor where I stood was divided into several large rooms. Each had a specific purpose: one for meals, one for recreation, and another where supplies were rationed.

It was the same... and this was what I had feared the most.

I had assumed that there would be something noticeably different that would make locating their food machine easy. This food source, if it existed, had to have been discovered recently. And if it did exist, why did it take the Blues so long to find and make use of it? I knew enough about the air machines to know that they could not be modified to create carbolyte. Even if their equipment could be altered, no clones had been designed with the knowledge to do so.

I then considered my options. Asking questions would reveal me and any action I took could give me away, so searching on my own would be dangerous, but it was my only choice. I decided to go to the recreation area and hope for a clue to verify the Blue's statement. If I felt I was being suspected, I would have to escape to warn the other Yellows. We would be forced to wage war with the Blues to secure their machines. Otherwise, we would wither away while they waited for us to become weak enough to attack.

If they did catch and kill me here, by the time the Yellows understood the danger they were in, it would be too late. The other Yellows needed this information to have any chance of surviving.

But if I could eliminate their food source now, it would ensure our survival.

I made my way to the recreation room, nodding as I passed several other Blues. If any suspected me, they showed no sign. I found a corner to sit and observe. Some Blues were exercising on fitness machines, while others were watching recorded news feeds from the old world. We did the same thing at the carbolyte plant. Looping the same information over and over again to pass the time placated the older clones, but it seemed that the younger ones like myself were losing the satisfaction this activity was supposed to provide. Neither was the future of any concern unless it pertained to prolonging our existence. For some of us, recreation was elusive. Work was all we had.

Before I reached the top of the stairs, a bell chimed. Over the factory's loudspeakers, a voice called out that the food would be dispensed early tonight. Every Blue in the recreational center stood and began marching towards the cafeteria. I shuffled in behind them, moving to the rear of the line. At home, meals were scheduled at the same time every day.

Changing the mealtime was not normal. It puzzled me. I decided at the very least I would try to find out the truth, then escape while the Blues waited for the carbolyte to drain into their bodies.

I took a seat nearest the exit of the cafeteria. There was something different about this room that set it apart from its Yellow equivalent, but I could not figure out what. The size seemed about the same, and the tables were arranged in similar linear rows. I noticed there were a few vacant seats scattered about. The seats back home were always filled at the feeding times. Meals usually began and ended on schedule, rarely taking any longer than ten minutes. A typical feeding would start with a ration of a single tube filled with liquid carbolyte that plugged directly into our biosuits. Then we sat and waited five minutes for the liquid nutrients to be completely processed.

I planned on pretending to plug in my carbolyte tube and wait for the others to be incapacitated by their feeding. Then I could leave the air factory and bring the sample back home to be compared with our own. If they were somehow producing their own carbolyte, there would have to be differences. Differences in a sample of the Blue carbolyte would confirm the machine's existence.

A clone in charge of serving the meal stood at the middle of each table. Instead of passing out the tubes of carbolyte, he set a large bucket down. Before I had a chance to see inside the bucket, every Blue in the cafeteria took the helmet off their biosuits.

At that moment, I realized I had failed and was seconds away from being caught. Their faces were identical to mine, save one major exception, one that would announce to all my allegiance. Every Blue bore scars of mutilation, likely inflicted by some sharp object. Deep grooves were carved in intricate patterns on all of their faces with no two that matched. I left my helmet on, and hundreds of sets of identical grey eyes turned to me. I was about to die.

A strong hand clasped my shoulder and I braced myself for the inevitable strike that would follow. Instead, the snaps on the back of my biosuit's helmet were loosened and the helmet removed, exposing my perfect features.

"Sit down and eat, comrade," a voice said. "We will speak afterwards."

I looked behind me, but the one that spoke was already walking away, carrying his own bucket.

Not a single Blue seemed to notice or care that an un-marked intruder was sitting among them. They reached into the buckets and took out things shaped and colored nothing like carbolyte.

A bucket was passed over to me. I put my hand into it. My fingers found something tube-shaped, but it was much larger and heavier than the carbolyte canisters. I pulled it out and placed it on the platter in front of me. There was no way that it would fit into the feeding connector of my biosuit.

I poked at it with my finger. "What is this?" I asked, my voice elevated. I was nervous, I realized. The thing was warm to the touch, even through my glove, a mishmash of brown, red, and black with white tips on the ends.

"Besides carbolyte, the only thing we can eat," one of the Blues said, not making eye contact. "Hurry up and finish it. The boss wants to speak with you."

"How do I ingest it?" I asked.

"Look around you. You eat it like the people of the old world, the ones that were not worker models. Just open your mouth, bite into it, chew, and then swallow."

"I know what those words mean," I said, "but why does it have to come this way? Why does it not plug in?"

"No more talking. The boss will explain. Eat."

I did as he directed. Pieces of it had to be torn off with the teeth and then converted into smaller portions I could swallow. It took its time to arrive at my stomach, unlike the carbolyte which raced through the body supplying instant gratification. The white portion in the food's center was a rod that I supposed had been used to grow it. I tried to eat it too, but was stopped by the Blue that had been instructing me.

"You are finished. I will take you to the boss now." He stood up and I followed him.

While we headed to the boss's chambers, a new thought came to me that offered a possible explanation for everything. Perhaps this boss belonged to the old race, someone who had somehow survived and knew secrets of food that were not programmed into the clones. Maybe the carved marks on their faces originated from the old world. The scars could serve some greater purpose that I did not yet understand. By the time we had reached the end of our walk, I had fully expected to be introduced to a survivor from The Reset.

My escort took me to a room—an office—located up the stairs, with a window overlooking the cafeteria. The back of a large chair was facing me and one of the food buckets was tipped over on a desk. Several of the white pieces in assorted shapes were strewn across the desktop. My escort stepped out of the office and the boss's chair swiveled toward me after his door shut.

"Would you believe that I knew you were a Yellow the moment you set the cart down in front of the factory?" I am sure my disappointment was apparent.

The boss was a clone too. His face, unlike the others' intricate designs, had a single, simple, diamond-shaped scar in the middle of his forehead. The skin had been removed to the bone.

"You had way too much product. The clone I sent out to meet you was not even supposed to get any carbolyte. Yet you come with your cart halfway full and drop it off and walk in."

"Why did you not stop me?" I asked. My eyes had been focusing on his scar the whole time and the ridges of flesh that outlined it.

"Because I wanted to observe you. To see what you were going to do. The Blue you killed told you that we had a new way to acquire food. You killed him to find out because your carbolyte would become worthless. Correct?"

"That is true."

He rubbed the mark on his head. "Of course it is. By the way you are looking at me I can tell that our marks are something you had not seen before coming here. I am going to assume that you smashed our trader's head in. That was why you did not see he had carved out his own identity. I made the markings mandatory as a way to spot spies. What I did not know then was that these marks gave us a new sense of purpose. That we should not all be the same. Identity, like your meal, is something we have been craving without even knowing we desired it."

He paused for a moment and stroked some of the white shapes covering his desk. "How did you like it, by the way?"

"It was... different, but in a good way. I feel better and more satisfied than I ever have before. How did you get your air machines to make it?"

"Our air machines did not make your meal. We did it ourselves."

"But how? What did you use? Was there something left over in your factory that made it?"

"There was and still is," he laughed—a sound I had never heard a clone produce before. It was threatening, beautiful, and terrifying all at once. "When The Reset happened, you know that our two factories were all that remained. You also know that everyone inside had been genetically engineered to thrive in an environment that no longer exists. The air we breathe has to be carbon treated, and carbolyte is heavily processed to best suit our nutritional requirements."

"So where does the new food come from?"

The boss continued, ignoring my question. "For years, I have asked myself this very question, a question I will now pose to you. If you answer correctly, you will live. Otherwise, you will die. Does this sound fair to you?"

He leaned forward in his chair, inches away from my face. There was a piece of his meal stuck between his front teeth that he flicked at with his tongue. He closed his mouth and made a slurping sound.

"It does not matter how it sounds to me," I said. "You are the boss."

"That is one good answer. You will live if your next is as good. Tell me, what is the only thing left in this world that is entirely manufactured? What is made in the factories besides air and carbolyte?"

I looked at the boss and looked at the shapes on his desk. I felt my own hands and squeezed them tightly. I suddenly knew what they were and what he wanted to hear.

"Clones... It is us... We are... We are the only created things left." The things on his desk took the shape of bones.

My interrogator bared his teeth and the piece of clone that had been lodged there was gone. The ends of his mouth curved. I realized he was smiling. I mimicked his movements and matched the expression. Stretching the corners of my face felt strange, but somehow natural.

"I am glad you can see that. I would like you to stay with me a little while longer. Join us. We are going to war soon. Between our cloning pods and air machines, we will not be short on resources. And when the Yellows submit or choke to death, we will take their plant and assimilate whatever is left."

"Why?" I asked. "You have already won. You have food, you have air. What else do you need?"

He paused. "More," was all he said, reaching into the bucket and drawing out another piece to eat. He offered it to me and I took it.

Our smiles never left our faces.

It has been four weeks since I joined the Blues and one week since we took the Yellow's carbolyte plant. I had carved my identity onto my face as soon as I knew what I wanted.

There are two long lines, one across my forehead and the other across my chin. On these lines, I have etched squares resembling teeth above my eyes and below my lips. It is the largest mark I have seen so far. We have integrated ourselves with several Yellows and are now no longer Blues or Yellows. Everyone is Green.

I have been put in charge of the carbolyte factory, which now pumps out enough food to feed both plants. I have tasked the youngest clones to find ways to create recreation for us to pass the time. One introduced a game that involves casting the painted knucklebones of past meals, based off something people in the old world once played. He called it Dominoes.

My desk overlooks the cafeteria. The Greens below are being served their meals. On my desk are three carbolyte packets that I have been ignoring. We have been trying to get back on carbolyte, because the cloning pods here are already exhibiting signs of breaking down. I have not told the Greens at the air plant this yet, but I will have to soon.

I want to use my jaw muscles. I want to rip and tear into my food, not sit down and plug it in. Below, the Greens all are ignoring the carbolyte, all of them except one, a former Yellow who was one of the older clones remaining at the factory. He tilts his head back as he begins the carbolyte digestion process, exposing the flesh of his neck. The Greens excuse themselves from the table and converge on that spot. Several have knives.

I leave my office, hoping there is something left by the time I get there.

Black

Ashley Norris Hurd

Blue. Yellow. Red.

She reached out her hand, hesitated, and drew it back.

Yesterday she chose Pink, her mind full of images of cotton candy and My Little Ponies.

The pain was excruciating. It ran through her veins like wildfire and melted her from the inside out. She had passed out screaming and woke up in a puddle of sweat and vomit.

Of course, that was gone now. Sucked through the floor by the vacuum tubes, these straw-like tunnels that somehow cleaned up every mess she made.

Blue. Yellow. Red.

Some days she pretended it didn't matter, that her fate was the same no matter the vial. Most days she forced herself to believe that her choice made a difference.

In this sterile room, with its dull white walls and fluorescent lights, nothing was under her control, not even her body once she took the vial.

Her choice was the only part of her life she could dictate.

The Sound was grating, like fingernails on a chalkboard shrieking across the room and drilling into her brain. If she didn't choose soon, it would only become louder.

Once she had waited an hour, it must have been an hour. She had put her hand to her ear, expecting to find blood, before she had driven the vial into the receptacle embedded in her arm.

That one had been Brown.

It had swelled her eyes shut and stretched her skin until she felt like it would burst. Sleep hadn't come that night, and she'd curled up in the corner, crying silent tears.

Blue. Yellow. Red.

Blue, like berries and the sky. She yearned to see the sky.

Yellow, sunshine and baby chicks. How long had it been since she touched something soft? Even her body had become rigid, mirroring the room that encased her.

Red. Blood. Chipped nail polish. Cherries.

A beep. A warning.

Blue. Yellow. Red.

She reached out, caressed the vials, grateful to touch something from outside the room.

Nail polish. She had loved nail polish. Every day a new color. Every day a new statement.

Red.

The tremors started in her hands. She watched them shake, fascinated by the lack of influence her mind had on her hands' movements.

As the shaking spread, she sunk to the floor.

Within minutes, she was sliding across the cold metal. Her limbs shoved her body from side-to-side as she concentrated on not biting her tongue.

Her head struck the wall, and the world faded to black. That was Red.

The broth was thin and tasted of boiled peas. A single sliver of carrot floated across the surface, taunting her with the illusion of solid food.

She had yet to determine who or what brought her food. A small door at the base of the wall offered her only clue. But it didn't open unless she was asleep, unconscious.

A whir, like winding up a toy car.

She knew what it meant. Maybe today she would take her time.

She licked the last drop of broth from the bowl, and set it in the corner. It always disappeared, no matter where she put it.

With the click of bones and a rasp of weak lungs, she stood.

Four steps. Eight from wall to wall. Four from her seat— the center—to the compartment.

Purple. Yellow. Black.

Sometimes one repeated. Repeated until she tried it.

Except Black.

Every ten days. Black. The only way to tell time.

Ten days. Twenty. Thirty. Forty. Fifty. Now sixty.

Sixty days.

And never Black.

Black meant darkness. How would she wake up from that?

Purple. Yellow. Black.

Her head still ached from Red. She couldn't take the Sound today. It would start soon.

Purple.

She'd always loved purple. Before.

But the last time had brought pain. The time before fear. Even further back, despair.

The illusions were the worst. She saw him, always him. And it tore her heart to pieces.

Yellow.

Yesterday's fare.

Would this vial do the same as yesterday's?

What if the repetition was mocking her, she wondered. Showing her what she should have chosen. Maybe Yellow would have saved her.

But that was yesterday. Today Yellow could hurt.

Black.

No. Not today.

The darkness would not take her yet.

Yellow.

Why not?

At first she was fine. She even began to hope. Today was the day, the day she would conquer the vial.

He came from the corner. She turned and he was there, walking towards her. His blond hair draped across his eyes, a half-smile teasing his lips.

He reached out his hand, reaching for her, desiring her. Her first love. Her only love. She hadn't had time for another.

His name stalled on her lips, unable to spill into the air. Unwilling to admit her mind was failing, wanting to believe he was there. Needing to believe.

She struggled to her knees, felt the bones digging into the floor, her skin too thin a barrier to make a difference.

Then his smile faded. She cowered.

Yellow was not hope, sunshine, or baby chicks.

She watched as the blood poured from his mouth, flowed down his chest. He fell to his knees, coughing and choking, dying another death just beyond her touch.

Afterward, she huddled in the corner, crying, his image stamped inside her eyelids.

Sleep came like a gift. A gift followed by a nightmare.

Brown. White. Orange.

Fate. Fate would decide.

She spun in a slow circle, eyes closed, arms outstretched, careful not to lose her balance.

Her fingers flitted across the vials, settled on one.

She withdrew it, thought about not looking.

But she had to know the color. How else to stay sane?

The colors were reality. The only thing that mattered from out there.

Brown.

Her mouth filled with a taste, the taste of chocolate. Rich and dark, she drank it in, wallowed in it, let it awaken her palate.

Too much.

Too much.

Too much.

She was choking, choking like him. She crumpled onto her knees, slamming them into the floor. The pain jolted her body as her hands grabbed her neck, groping for a way to end it.

She coughed, throat burning, and doubled over.

Her lungs emptied. Her breath had been stolen.

As consciousness left, her last thought was of the cruelty of Brown.

No food. The first time in sixty-one days.

Were they done with her? Was her punishment over?

Then a whir. A click.

Her stomach roiled as she crawled forward.

Pink. Peach. Tan.

Such pretty colors, light pastels that would've made her smile. Before.

She'd been laughing when they had come for her. The Gray Men.

Gray steel. Gray clothes. Gray guns. Gray faces.

She hadn't expected to lose color that day, lose it except for the vials. She now lived in a world of white guarded by gray. Only the vials broke the monotony.

She reached for Peach, thinking of a juicy sweetness bursting in her mouth and dribbling down her chin. A hair's breadth from the vial, she stopped.

A voice. The first one she'd heard since the Gray Men led her away while her friends screamed in terror.

"Subject 80584. Is it ready?"

She strained her ears, sticking the side of her head into the vial compartment as far as it could go.

The distinctive clack of a clipboard. The hollow thump of a Gray Man's step.

"Did you give her Tan?"

Retreating footsteps answered. Real ones with heels, so unlike a Gray Man's heavy tread.

She slid to the floor and clutched her ankles.

Tan.

Why Tan?

Did they mean for her to hear those words?

Would Tan be her salvation?

Would Tan be her doom?

Minutes passed, minutes in which her mind changed its decision a billion times.

What did they want her to do? What did she want to do?

She'd do anything if it would end this.

She peered into the compartment cavity.

Pink. Peach. Tan.

She glided her fingers across the vials, seeking some hint toward the right choice.

Did she have anything left to lose?

Tan.

The heat invaded her senses before she opened her eyes. It pounded against her eyelids, sizzled the tips of her fingers and bottoms of her feet. She woke screaming.

Blazing light emanated from every corner, every nook, every cranny. It blasted her vision, causing her to see vivid lines across her eyes. The heat came from the light, stinging her sensitive skin.

She tried to back away, tried to sit up, tried to scramble across the floor into the corner.

She was tied down with thick straps buckled around her wrists, ankles, chest, and waist. She strained against them, but tired quickly without results.

Not vial Red, but the red of flames, fire, and flares. Invading every one of her senses. Making her scream and strain against the unyielding shackles.

She fought to stay awake, fought against the pain. She knew the restraints meant something. This was her test. Her test was to stay conscious. What else could it be?

She tried to trick herself. Just another minute. And then another minute. Then the pain became too much and it was thirty seconds. Then a minute. She counted out the seconds, inserting random words between the numbers.

One pineapple two frog three tricycle four pyramid.

Just another forty-five seconds.

The red went away. It coiled away from her, snaked into crevices, and darted into cracks.

The red went away.

The door swung open. She had not realized there was a door—its edges had blended seamlessly into the tiled walls.

A Gray Man entered. He was tall, broad-shouldered with a blank face and stiff limbs. His cold fingers wrapped around her arm. His other hand swung forward. He held a syringe that he plunged into her arm. She glanced at the liquid as it streamed into her body.

Silver.

She awoke shivering. Her meager clothes were gone, the jeans and sweater she had worn since her first day here. They had faded and torn. But they were all she had left.

All she thought she'd had left.

She lifted her head to search the familiar white room. Surely, they had left her clothes.

Her head was too light. No strands swayed against her cheek, cascaded down her shoulders.

Her hand trembled as she raised it, rubbed it over the baby smoothness of her skull.

She bawled. It echoed off the walls and back at her. It mocked her as it filled the room with a never-ending cry.

When her throat had turned raw, she collapsed into the corner.

Tears ran down her cheeks, dripping onto her bare belly.

She'd thought she had nothing to lose when she chose Tan.

She was wrong.

Naked and alone, without any connection to her old life, her old self, she descended into despair.

Her clenching stomach and parched throat marked the passing of time.

No vials came.

No food appeared.

Her despair swallowed her whole.

A whir. A click.

Too feeble to stand up, she pivoted her body, her bones grinding, until she could see the opposite wall.

Vials. She could just discern the light reflecting off their glass casings.

Without debate, she knew her choice.

With grasping fingers she pulled herself across the room.

Her body felt like a shell, a skeleton. Her skin white as paper, the veins throbbing under the surface.

She counted the distance.

Eight feet, seven, six.

Her breath came in gasps.

Five, four, three.

Her arms and legs twitched, not used to the movement.
Two.

She was taking too long. The Sound would start soon,
the screeching she was certain would shatter her skull.

One.

She still couldn't stand. After several agonizing seconds,
she managed to extend her arm, blindly clasping a vial with
her fingers.

Grape.

She could end it here. Just let her frail fingers make the
choice for her.

But she so pined for color, yearned for control, craved
something tangible.

She reached again.

Macaroni and cheese.

And again.

Burnt toast.

She smiled at the choice. What could be simpler?

Macaroni and cheese.

She waited, waited for hours.

Nothing.

No pain, no hallucinations, no noise, no sickness.

Nothing.

Sleep for once came easy.

Clothes. Under the vial compartment, a neat stack.

Loose pants, a cami, a cardigan. All white.

She slipped them on, savored their softness.
Her skin felt less fragile when covered with cotton.

The aroma caught her attention first.
She pulled herself to the bowl of broth.
Picked it up, hands quivering.
It tasted better than macaroni and cheese.

Days passed. Days of nothing, no matter the color.
Her nerves evaporated.
Her body began to form again into a person.
Finally, she was able to stand.

Red. Brown. White.
She smiled as her fingers traced the vials.
Her new game was to associate the vials with a little piece
of herself.
Red. Her lips.
Brown. The stubble on her scalp.
White. Her skin.
Red.

Startled, she sat down abruptly, crashing onto the floor.
Warmth, warmth she was sure would turn into fire.
She pressed into the wall, kneading her hands, waiting
for the pain to start.
The warmth spread, stretching down her arms, sinking
into her toes. And it stayed.
Stayed warm. Stayed pleasant. Stayed comforting.
Stayed until she slept.

White. Green. Blue.

Could she hope for another day like yesterday?

Or another day of nothing?

She picked up White, then put it back. Did this once more.

Green.

Her senses were dancing, alive with smells and tastes and sounds.

A feast.

She could smell the apple pie, taste the cranberries, hear the crinkle of tin foil.

She lay, content, as her hunger waned.

Hours of smell, taste, and sound were enough.

Days passed. Each one brought a new delight—

Yellow. A multisensory road trip with her parents.

White. Tiny movies playing inside her eyelids.

Orange. A vivid tide of flavors of sugary confections.

Blue. Snow crunching beneath her favorite boots.

Purple. Music swirling throughout her brain, her lips mouthing the words then belting them out.

She forgot pain, forgot fear, forgot anxiety.

The white room became a sanctuary, her salvation.

A whir. A click.

She pranced across the room, eager for today's choices.

Pink: bubblegum and tutus.

Lilac: the scent of summer.

Tan.

Tan

The memory came flooding back. It barreled through her brain and exploded.

The words spoken outside her door.

The sizzling. The straps. The silver stream.

Tan.

She drew breaths in gulps as she stumbled backward.

Tan. Tan. Tan. Tan. Tan. Tan. Tan. Tan. Tan. Tan.

She hammered her fists against the floor until the skin broke and sprayed the tiles with red.

She screamed obscenities, pleaded for guidance.

Tan.

When the Sound started, she barely registered its importance.

Then it was ricocheting across the room, clawing into her ears, forcing her to choose.

She sprung to her feet and staggered to the vials.

She'd choose what they least expected her to.

Tan.

Then, nothing.

With a relieved sigh she awoke. She shook off Tan.

Today would be better. The test was over. Maybe today she would hear an orchestra, or relive a picnic with her love.

A whir. A click.

She crossed the room. Ready.

Tan. Amber. Bronze.

Never before was a color offered again the day after it was taken. But here was Tan.

They were violating their own rules. Rules she had put her faith in.

Defiance roared up inside her.

Bronze.

Nothing.

Anticipation. Apprehension. She remained in the corner until the Sound started.

Yesterday's nothing wasn't a gift. It was a taunt.

A promise of pain.

She closed her eyes and stuck out a hand. She stopped when it hit the wall. Slowly, so slowly, she reopened her eyes and looked down.

Tan. Gold. Tan.

Tan. Gold. Tan.

Never did a color repeat within the vials.

Her semblance of control, her feeling of serenity were slipping away.

She had no choice.

Gold.

The best vial yet. She felt as if she were floating on a cloud. She danced across the room as music billowed around her. And when she closed her eyes, she could see them. Her friends. They were laughing and dancing with her. For hours she swayed, completely lost. Completely happy.

She woke, refreshed and reinvigorated.

Today's vials would surely bring her nice dreams and fun things. Gold had convinced her. Gold had been perfect.

A whir. A click.

She rose deliberately and strode to the vials.

She imagined the colors as she walked, debated the possibilities. She would relish this choice, choose just before the Sound.

Tan. Tan. Tan.

What had happened to Gold? To Bronze? To Yellow? Or Red? Green? Purple?

How could she choose from a trio of monotony?

How would she know the effect of her choice?

How could she keep any control?

How could she choose?

Tan. Tan. Tan.

She curled into a ball as the Sound started. It amplified rapidly, screeching, hurting. She covered her ears and lay absolutely still, unable to rise and choose.

Not choose. No choice.

Her head pounded, her consciousness splintered as the Sound increased in volume and pitch. Her vision faded in and out, in and out. She was screaming, screaming with the Sound, trying and failing to drown it out. She quaked and sobbed, terrified to choose.

No choice.

The Sound seared into her, became part of her.
She drowned in it.

No whir. No click. Just the vial drawer opening.
Confused, she crossed the room.
The silence was too much.
She snatched up the vials, ignoring the colors, and hurled them down.
They all shattered, the glass strewn across the floor, the colors trickling outward.
The *color.*
Tan.

She hadn't moved. She sat frozen among the vials' ruins in her newfound silence.
The compartment opened in her peripheral vision.
Mechanically, she struggled to get to her feet, devoid of emotion, shocked into indifference.
It slid easily into the receptacle in her arm. She watched with detached fascination as it stained her veins.
Only then did she realize its significance.
Her final choice.
Black.

Homecoming

James Austin McCormick

Certain personality types don't at all mind the convalescing process. I'm not one of them. The couple of weeks lying in bed hooked up to tubes and half a dozen monitors hadn't been fun. But when your nervous system collapses from total catatonic shock you don't take chances. I'd been clinically dead for seven minutes, the doctors told me. They could run all the damn tests they wanted.

It also gave me a chance to think. I was here because someone had tried to hack into my brain while I'd been on-line and install a command there. Luckily the cerebrochip I'd been testing threw a firewall up. It saved me from the attack but nearly killed me in the process.

"What do you want to do now, boss?" Brogan, my company's chief tech, asked as he folded the paper that contained the data simulation of the attack. I sat up in bed. My body still ached.

"You still can't trace the sender?" I asked.

Brogan shook he head.

"Nothing. No trail of any kind."

I ran a hand over four days of stubble.

"Well, whoever it was went to a lot of trouble breaking through our security. They won't have given up." I swung my legs over the side of the bed. My feet throbbed as blood began to pump back into them.

"I need to be prepared," I said. I touched the base of my skull. It was still tender. "We should add some new features to the cerebrochip, but more importantly, we redesign the firewall."

Brogan nodded. "Any ideas?" he asked.

I nodded. "Plenty."

Sian took me home the next morning. Even on the drive back I could tell something was wrong. My wife normally did the talking for the both of us, but now she was quiet. I could barely raise a smile from her. Something was on her mind. A couple of times I thought she came close to telling me what it was, but then seemed to think better of it. But I wasn't the type to push. If she wanted to open up to me she would.

A few days later the call came. Sian picked it up. She listened for a bit, brushing her long, dark hair away from her pale cheek, then held the phone out to me.

"It's your father," she said.

The announcement took me by surprise. For a moment I was too stunned to do anything but stare back at her. I'd had a puzzle in my head for over two weeks. Now the first piece of it had slotted into place.

Sian misread my reaction as one of reluctance and threw me a pleading look.

"Please," she whispered, pressing the receiver into my hand. "It's serious."

Before I could answer, she turned and left. My hand trembled slightly as I put the phone to my ear.

"I can't believe your father lives on Eden!" Sian said, her voice little more than a gasp as I sent the craft high into the sky.

I gave a shrug. "Where else would one of the elite live?" I said. "Besides, it's just a place, like anywhere else."

Sian smiled. "No, Alex," she replied, shaking her head. "Nowhere's like Eden!"

I didn't answer. Nothing, it seemed, would dampen her enthusiasm about seeing the floating city. Her whole mood had changed the moment I'd agreed to the visit. She glanced at me, the smile still on her face.

"This break will be good for you," she said. "You work way too hard." She rubbed my arm. "I've hardly seen you the last few days. What have you and Brogan been working on in that lab?"

I shrugged again. From the moment I had taken the call I'd begun preparing for this encounter with my father. I wondered what Sian would do if I told her the truth about what was happening—beg me to turn back or urge me to carry on. Looking at her now I thought I knew answer. I hoped I was wrong.

We left the holographic freeway and headed towards the city in the clouds.

"Do you hate your father?" my wife asked me, gazing up at the billowing white. "You never talk about him."

"Hate's too a simple word," I told her, "to describe what I feel." I looked at her. I wanted her so much to understand.

"My father isn't a good man," I continued. "I have spent my life trying to help others. He…" I shook my head. "Trust me, he serves only one master. Himself."

She placed a hand to my cheek. "It'll be okay," she said, her voice soft and reassuring.

"You don't get it," I said, trying to keep the irritation out of my voice. "He's dangerous, Sian. Promise me you won't be taken in by him." I stared into her emerald eyes. She coloured a bit, then nodded.

"I promise you," she said. I must have appeared less than convinced because she leaned forward. "I promise," she repeated, kissing me gently on the cheek.

"Okay then," I said. "Hang on." I sent the craft sweeping above the airborne city. As I did, a series of laser canons at the perimeter swivelled in our direction.

Sian shot me a worried expression.

"Relax," I told her. "I have a clearance code. Of course if it's incorrect then we'll end up as ions drifting in the breeze."

I hit the seven digit number I had pre-programmed into the comm system. A moment later the cannons retracted.

The craft cleared the perimeter and began to soar over the cyclopean, white marble palaces and expanses of ornate Grecian gardens. Sian stared in awe. The aesthetic was indeed incredible, but I reminded myself that behind the façade was something very unpleasant. This was the personal paradise of people who had done terrible things to be here.

The craft's nav system blinked as we passed over a large lake of blue crystal and started to descend automatically. As we closed in I could make out a small island in the middle of the water and at its centre a dark structure that reminded me of a medieval fortress. The craft veered abruptly and aimed for a blue neon-lit launch pad atop one of its towers.

A tall, bone white servant who moved a bit too stiffly to be human waited for us there. As we stepped out of our craft, a bitter, icy wind greeted us, yet the tall figure seemed impervious to the elements.

"I am Talbot, the butler" he said, his voice clipped and perfectly enunciated. "The master of the house wishes me to convey his greetings to you both."

I felt a knot of fear clench in my stomach. It was too late to go back now.

"And where is the master?" I asked, trying to maintain a semblance of calm.

"Receiving medical treatment at the moment," the butler said, "but he hopes he'll be sufficiently recovered to join you for the evening meal later." He clapped his hands together and two spider-like machines jumped out from nowhere and scurried over to the craft, lifting our luggage onto their segmented backs.

"If you will follow me," Talbot said, "I will show you to your quarters." He turned and walked towards a transparent domed structure a short distance away. Inside, an elevator waited to take us down. The metal insects skittered after him.

Sian hesitated, her eyes fixed on the giant arachnids.

"Relax," I told her. "They won't hurt you. At least, not yet."

Our room was spacious enough for a family of five to live in and crammed with every luxury imaginable. A large red optisphere on a titanium tentacle dropped down from the ceiling as we entered. It welcomed us in a warm tone and then promised to execute any commands we should have. I imagined my father's malign eye on the other end, observing us. I ignored the strange device.

"So here we are," I said. "Inside a grand castle on top of a billion tonnes of levitating rock." I glanced at Sian. "How does it feel?"

"Scary," she answered. "What keeps it up here?"

"That's their big secret," I told her. "My theory is electro-magnetism. Somehow they've polarised the rock so it repels the earth's magnetic core. I've had our company carry out similar experiments but none were ever successful."

I surveyed the chamber. Luxurious as it was, the very last thing I could do now was relax. I had to acquire a complete layout of the mansion, work out just what surprises the old man had in store for us. If anything went awry I would need to get out of here in a hurry.

"I'm going to take a look around," I said, sliding a pen-shaped scanner from my pocket. With any luck I could use it to build a 3D profile of the place. I took a couple of steps towards the door.

The crimson optisphere darted in front of me.

"May I be of service?" it inquired in its mellow voice.

"Yeah," I said. "How about getting the hell out of my way?"

"Alex, look at this!"

I whirled around and saw Sian standing beside a jumbo Jacuzzi.

"I just hit this button and…" She waved a hand at the bubbling water and began to strip off her clothes.

"Come on," she said. "What do you say? We could both do with a soak."

"Maybe later," I replied, turning back to the luminous mechanical eye blocking my way. The thing hung there a few moments then moved aside.

"Start without me," I told Sian and ventured outside.

The dining area was this massive circular chamber with bronze walls embedded with bizarre insectoid sculptures. By the stairwell was a huge figure of a centipede, coiled with its metal fangs ready to strike. Sian glanced uneasily around the room, then finally turned back to me.

"Has he got a thing for bugs?"

"He developed these things for the military," I explained. "Perfect killing machines. I guess he's just a proud father."

Sian regarded me for a moment. "Do you think he could have changed?" she asked. "You said he's done a lot of bad things, but that was before. I mean, he's dying now. That can change someone's perspective, yes?" She leaned forward and when she spoke again it was in a whisper. "And he's chosen this moment to ask you here."

I saw the flash of greed in Sian's eyes and wondered if I had ever really known this woman.

A booming chime resonated throughout the chamber and we realised Talbot had entered the room. He stood beside a gigantic bronze gong.

"Thank you for waiting," he said. As he spoke a host of spiders scurried out, each one conveying a different dish to the table.

At the far end of the chamber, twin doors parted and a crouched, silhouetted figure made its way down the murky corridor towards us. It was my father.

It had been more than two decades since I'd last seen him and I had destroyed any photos of him that remained with me. I had no idea what he looked like anymore. The last memory I had was of a tall, robust man with a neat, greying beard and very dark, slicked hair. He must have been in his fifties then, but had appeared much younger. I remember my mother telling me stories about how he'd spent millions on drugs and treatments trying to stay young. Beginning to understand his character, even at that age, I suspected he was striving for more than that. He had planned to outlive us all.

It was a surprise then when the frail figure, slumped in a hoverchair, entered the chamber. At first I could make little out as the edges of the huge hall were in shadow, but as he emerged into the light the full extent of his condition became evident.

The image of him I'd carried all those years bore scant resemblance to the individual that presented itself now.

The dark hair had grown long and gone white. His now clean-shaven face was gaunt, the paper-thin flesh sunken inwards beneath his prominent check bones. Yet the skin was strangely pink and unlined and as he passed under the chandelier, it looked more like wax than flesh. All his wealth, all his power hadn't protected him from this.

The old man took his place at the head of the long, smoked glass table. He set down his silver-tipped cane in front of him and regarded us for a long time. His once bright blue eyes were now dull and glassy. Finally he smiled, but very little of that waxwork face moved.

"Hello Alex," he said, his voice unexpectedly strong in comparison to his ailing frame. "You've grown into quite the handsome man, I see. And an influential one too. I hear your companies lead the field in virtual technologies." He nodded approvingly. "And you direct much of your resources into helping the poor and less fortunate."

"I believe the privileged have a duty to help their fellow man," I replied, "rather than exploit them."

The old man smiled. "A noble sentiment." He was silent for a moment then grasped his goblet.

"Well, I would like to thank you and your beautiful..." He cast a questioning gaze at Sian.

"Wife," she said, somewhat shyly. "We'd gotten married a couple of months ago."

The old man smiled again. "How charming," he said. "I'd like to thank you and your beautiful wife for coming, Alex. It was more than I had a right to expect." He took a deep breath and raised his goblet. "If you don't mind, I would like to propose a toast." He grinned at us. "To homecomings."

My fingers lingered around my drink. I felt Sian's foot touch mine, urging me to pick it up.

"Is there something wrong?" the old man asked, catching my hesitation. "I assure you it is excellent wine." There was a hint of amusement in his voice. "I'm not in the habit of poisoning my guests."

I picked up the goblet and ran it under my nose. My father threw a look at Sian, who immediately coloured.

"Alex, please," she whispered into my ear. "You're embarrassing me."

"And we wouldn't want to do that, would we?" Satisfying myself, I put the goblet to my lips. I took a sip but didn't repeat the old man's toast.

"I'm sure you have many questions," my father said after we had set our drinks down on the table again. I leaned back in my chair and frowned.

"Questions? Not really."

The old man studied me with unblinking eyes.

"You think you know all about me, Alex?" he said, his voice benign. I studied his ancient face in return.

"No," I replied, "but I know enough. I know you kept my mother a prisoner in our home for the first ten years of your marriage, then had her committed to an asylum when she tried to leave you. Because you couldn't risk a divorce. Altus Industries was her inheritance after all."

I glided my hand along the faint crescent scar on my cheek. "And I know you gave me this at her funeral."

Sian, who'd been an awkward observer until now, tilted her head. She directed a dubious look at the old man.

"Would you like to tell her?" I asked.

My father steepled his gnarled fingers under his chin. "Please," he said, with a wave of his hand. I nodded.

"My mother didn't kill herself," I went on. "I'm certain of it and there was only one person who ever benefited from her death." My eyes locked with the old man's. "I told him as much when we were sitting in the limo on the ride back. And he used that on me." I indicated the silver-tipped cane beside him.

He nodded. "I have done some terrible things, Alex, for which I am truly sorry. But I swear to you, I had nothing to do with your mother's death." He paused, taking another tiny sip of his wine. His eyes flitted to Sian for a moment.

"I can't make right what I did," he continued, "but I do want to try and atone for it. I doubt if I have more than a few days left. The doctors call it photonic induced myelin decay. The apparent consequence of an energy transfer experiment I undertook some years ago. And now that my time is so very short I have given a lot of thought to my legacy.

"I have been a very successful man. A powerful one too. And as you suggested some moments ago, Alex, I have not always used that power for the good of my fellow man."

I didn't waste any effort pointing out what an under-statement this was. Altus Industries had their insidious claws deep into the underworld. My own researches had revealed links to kidnapping, murder, organ trafficking, even illegal gene mutations in human DNA. There was much more, of course, but he concealed his tracks well, and an outsider, even one with resources like mine, could only uncover so much.

The old man snapped his fingers and Talbot produced a slim folder. He walked around the table and laid it out before me. I flicked it open.

"I'm leaving everything to you, Alex," he announced.

Sian's breath quickened and out of the corner of my eye I saw her tongue dart across her lips.

"All you need do is sign."

Talbot proffered me a pen, but I didn't take it.

"Just think of all the people you can help," the old man pressed on, more forceful this time. "You *must* sign."

I shook my head. "I need time to think," I said, aware that I still hadn't had an opportunity to analyze the data I'd collected earlier. I couldn't make my move until I did. The old man looked less than pleased. Sian took my arm.

"Sweetheart," she said in an anxious voice. "What are you doing?"

"Very well," the old man said. "You may have the night to sleep on it. My lawyers arrive tomorrow."

As I finished evaluating the downloaded data from the scanner, I felt another ball of fear growing in the pit of my stomach. The old man's technology was beyond anything I had imagined. I knew he had stolen secrets from my companies before, but the level of espionage must have gone far deeper than any of us had guessed.

Nearly every piece of virtual technology I had developed was in the old man's possession. Who was to say he didn't also have a cerebrochip?

If he did I no longer had the advantage.

And then it struck me. I'd been crazy to try to take on someone as powerful and devious as my father. And now my time was running out. If I didn't get out of here tonight then the man named Alex Kubo would no longer exist this time tomorrow. The old man suspected I was not going to sign.

Something would be coming for me in the night. After I was gone it would be simple enough to forge my signature and simpler still to bribe the fat lawyers.

I paced up and down the bedroom calculating my next course of action. I gazed upon Sian's beautiful, peaceful face as she slept. I had a decision to make. Would I take her with me or not? I wanted to, desperately, but could I trust her anymore?

"Wake up," I said, joggling her shoulder. She murmured something and turned to me. Her lids parted a fraction and she regarded me with torpid eyes.

"What?" she said, her voice raspy.

"I know you went behind my back, Sian," I said. "Talking with the old man. Putting pressure on me to come here. He used you when he wasn't able to install the command himself during the virtual attack."

Her eyes widened. "Alex, I—"

"Don't deny it," I said. "I logged the call destinations to here."

Sian nodded. "Yes. It's true. But Alex, he wants to leave you everything. Imagine the life we could have."

I leaned forward, my face inches away from hers. "Did you know he was behind the attack?"

She winced as my fingers dug into her shoulders.

"No," she whimpered. "Of course not. Alex, what is this all about?"

I peered into those soft green eyes of hers.

"Go get dressed," I told her at last. "We're getting out of here." I flung the covers off her and dropped them onto the floor.

"Why?" she asked, sitting up and swinging her long legs over the side of the bed.

I was already pulling my jacket from its hanger. From the pocket I dug out my wallet and from it slid the prototype scanner card Brogan and I had developed, a rush job. I ripped off the thin plastic cover that disguised it as an ID card.

That was all the software I would require. Now I needed the hardware. I reached up and took down Sian's beauty bag from the shelf, unzipped it and emptied the contents onto the bed. I picked up her hairdryer, slipped the handle's panel off, and inserted an energy cell I'd designed to look like a make-up compact. I held up the makeshift energy weapon for inspection. It would do. If I'd attempted to smuggle any more firepower inside, the old man would have found out. I had no doubt he had scanners placed at every entrance.

Sian, who'd put on a pair of jeans, stared at me. "Alex," she said, panicked. "Answer me! Why are we doing this?"

I spun round. "Because the old man's going to erase me," I told her. "I thought I could take him on, but I can't."

She frowned. "Kill you? But you're his heir."

I shook my head. "I don't have time to explain. I told you before you can't trust him, Sian. If you don't believe me then go back to sleep. But I'm getting out of here while I still can."

She was silent for a moment, then nodded.

I went to the door and tried the lock. As I'd guessed, it wouldn't open.

"Magnetically sealed," I said. "The bastard's not taking any chances." I brandished my scanner card. "But I have a few tricks." I swiped the card down the jamb of the door, planted an ear to the panel, and heard a click. I gave a grunt of satisfaction. The card had passed its first real-world test, successfully scanning the door's electronic code then issuing a pulse command for the mechanism to unlock.

I opened the door and almost immediately half a dozen cybernetic arachnids appeared, scampering across the walls and ceiling.

"Close your eyes," I instructed Sian as I raised the blaster. I adjusted the setting to a wide dispersal beam and averted my face. A single shot was enough to turn the creatures into a cloud of minuscule fragments.

I waited, knowing it would take only moments for the security system to register that the sentries had gone offline. And seconds later, a black spherical droid, its scanner beams sweeping the area, swooped down the hallway to investigate. I pushed the door shut again. I heard the droid slow briefly as it passed our room, then continue on its journey in search of the missing sentinels.

We moved into the hall as soon as it was safe. My plan was to make it up to the roof as fast as possible. It didn't take long for me to realise something was very wrong.

"What is it?" Sian asked as I strode to the edge of the banister that circled the upper floor.

"The layout's changed," I answered. "The whole floor has retracted."

I underestimated the old man once again. I had thought I could dodge his net but he was way ahead of me. And it looked now like he'd decided to play one of his sick games too. He wanted to have some sport with me before the kill.

I indicated the spiral steps that ran along the wall.

"We have to take the stairwell."

I led Sian over to the stairs and set an experimental foot on the first step. Nothing happened. Sian started forwards but I stopped her.

"It's not going to be that easy," I told her. I held my palm out over the banister, close enough for my body heat to carry to the surface. A series of wicked skewers, each half an inch long, sprang up.

"Stay behind me," I said, placing a hand between the spikes as we began to ascend the stairs.

I proceeded carefully, expecting every step to activate another one of my father's nasty little surprises. But he had saved the next one until we reached the upper floor.

As soon as I laid a foot onto the walkway the whole place shuddered. Scratching noises rang out from the walls as the arachnids embedded within them stirred to life. In moments a sea of the creatures swarmed towards us.

But that wasn't the worst of the dangers. Below I saw the gigantic centipede animate. It travelled swiftly at us, scaling the wall with its many clawed limbs.

I jumped back just in time to avoid its razor sharp jaws and fired off a laser shot. The beam obliterated the head but the creature still functioned, arching its pitchfork-like tail, ready to strike.

"This way!" I yelled, pulling Sian towards the open doorway at the far end. A bejewelled wall lamp with red ruby eyes pivoted as it watched us pass.

The door slammed shut. When I reached for the handle, the surface morphed into a disfigured face. A hideous mouth yawned and a barbed metal tongue lashed out, wrapping itself around my wrist. I sliced through it with one well-placed shot. It proved an agonising experience to hurriedly prize the thing from my flesh.

I kicked the door open and hustled Sian through. Behind us the arachnids were pouring over the sides of the staircase. I tried to fire a wide dispersal beam at them but my weapon was out of power. I hit the recharge pad. It wouldn't be much good anymore, but would at least be able to build up enough energy for one more shot.

"Which way now?" Sian asked as I secured the door from the other side. I indicated the neon lit elevator shaft.

"My father wants us to go this way, of course," I said, placing the scanner card against the console. "But let's see if I can't throw my own surprise in there." A photon decrypter read the digital commands on the card's magnetic strip.

"Voice command," I said, overriding the system's program. I brought the elevator up, stopping it right before it reached our floor.

"Open doors," I commanded. The clear plastisteel cover slid back. I leapt onto the top of the elevator and beckoned Sian.

"Come on," I said. "It won't take long for those things to get through the door."

She stepped over beside me. "Up," I ordered. We were just in time—the arachnids came crashing through and began hurling themselves against the metalized glass.

"It's okay," I reassured, seeing the terror in Sian's eyes. "Nothing's getting through plastisteel."

I almost thought we were going to make it up to the roof, yet at the very last moment my command was overridden. The elevator suddenly veered sideways, transporting us into an incredible chamber that my scan had failed to detect. It looked as if it were constructed from interlocking mechanical systems. The domed interior gave the impression you were standing inside a vast machine.

At the far end an enormous crystal screen flared on. Tiny coloured points swirled about in chaotic orbits, gradually forming a hazy image. A silhouette floated out in front of it.

"Alex," a familiar voice said. "Did you really think you could run from me?" A photo cube suspended from a cord overhead blazed, illuminating the area. My father leaned forward in his hoverchair. A guttural laugh escaped his feeble chest.

"I did enjoy watching you, though," he added with a curl of his bloodless lips. "It's such a shame I don't have the time to really enjoy myself. You can't imagine the delights this house has waiting for the unsuspecting guest." He smiled as if recalling some amusing instances.

I stared at the decrepit, crippled figure and realised that no matter how long I lived, I would never loathe anyone as much as I did this evil old man.

I glanced at my blaster. The cells had recharged. I raised the weapon and aimed it squarely at him. Sian looked on in horror.

"Alex," she yelled, "No!"

I squeezed the last drop of energy from the weapon. A silver-blue bolt shot across the chamber, striking its target in the middle of the chest. The electrical discharge spread out, ripples spreading like clawing fingers over the emaciated frame. The flesh melted away from the skull like wax. But instead of revealing charred muscle and bone, I found myself gazing upon a mass of circuits and metal. Green eyes glowed at me for a few seconds and then faded. The head flopped forward.

I chucked the spent blaster aside.

"Show yourself, you coward!" I shouted.

"But Alex," the old man's voice answered, "I have been here all the time." The distorted image on the screen finally resolved itself into the face of my father.

The android in the chair slumped forward and collapsed onto the ground. Black, acrid smoke drifted up from its scorched circuits.

My eyes darted around the chamber, realisation dawning on me. The room was indeed a machine, specially designed to keep one man's mind alive. The monstrous eyes on the screen watched me keenly.

"You're a ghost," I said.

"You always were such a smart boy," my father replied. "I exist now purely as energy patterns, my mind running through the systems and circuits of this house."

"How long have you been dead?" I asked.

"Several weeks now. But I had to make sure everything was in place before I called you here." His lip twisted into a cruel sneer. "You had good reason to be suspicious of me, Alex. But I hardly think you could have predicted what it was I really wanted from you... although I suspect you do now."

I stared back at the smug features and inside breathed a sigh of relief. For once my father was not a step ahead of me. I *had* guessed what the old man was after, long before I had ever stepped foot onto Eden, and with Brogan's help had prepared for this fight.

Sian crept up behind me, laying a hand on my shoulder.

"What does he want?" she asked.

The old man raised an amused eyebrow. "I need a body, my dear," he said. "Your husband's, to be exact." Sian gasped.

"It's called digital induced possession," I explained to her. "An imprint of one cognitive system over another. No one's been able to do it yet, but he must have managed to create a prototype. I'm impressed."

"Thank you, Alex," the pixelated face said. "Though I must confess much of the information was stolen from your company's database."

The ground rumbled as segmented sections of the floor began to retract.

"Now, let's get started, shall we?"

Cables ripped free of their moorings overhead and coiled themselves around my limbs. I struggled but it was a futile gesture. They lifted me into the air. The metal bit so tightly into my flesh I could feel the blood dribbling down my arms.

A large hexagonal opening appeared in the centre of the floor and a large casket, resting on a glasslike column, rose up through it. Talbot, his machine servant, stood beside a nearby console.

The cables carried me towards the casket. The android went to hit the console.

"Stop!" my father ordered. Talbot froze.

"I believe Sian should be the one to do that," he said. His gigantic eyes turned to her. Sian took a step forward, then hesitated.

"You do want to live up here, don't you?" the old man asked. "Amongst the clouds?"

Her lip trembled. She glanced at me then at the screen.

The digital face scowled. "I'm not a patient man," the old man continued, his voice brimming with menace.

Sian's eyes welled with tears but finally she nodded.

"I'm sorry, Alex," she said, unable to look at me this time, "but this is… everything I've ever wanted."

She shuffled toward the console and slammed her palm down onto it. The casket hissed and its curved lid slid open. Emerald light spilled out from inside and dozens of luminous claws writhed towards me.

"Why him?" Sian asked. Her tone was sad but there was no hint of challenge in it.

"The best hosts are those with compatible DNA," the old man answered as the cables started to lower me into place. "The risk is too great otherwise."

The claws seized me, manoeuvring my body so that I was held fast, facing up. The casket lid slid back into position, sealing me within it. I found myself staring into a series of stroboscopic panels. A segmented metal arm reared up and its tip split apart, revealing thousands of microscopically thin tendrils. The tiny cilia rooted themselves into my skull.

My head exploded with crystalline flashes as another mind collided with my own. My whole being quaked with revulsion as my father's vile essence began to seep into me.

"Don't fight this, Alex," he said as I thrashed against my restraints. "It will only make the transfer more painful." As he spoke I could sense the malign pleasure in him. The old man wanted me to fight. It would make the game all that more enjoyable. Well, I had prepared for this and he would get the fight he desired.

But it would be a far different one than he expected.

The first thing I had to do was decrease my heart rate, bringing my autonomic nervous system under conscious control. Despite the physical discomfort I forced myself to breath slowly and deeply, letting the air fill my lungs.

The pounding in my ears subsided by degrees and finally I began to experience a level of calm. It was now time to spring the trap.

I visualised myself in the centre of a dark void, empty of everything apart from my being. An alien glow tried to fill the darkness but I willed it away. In its stead I created spheres of radiant energy that were an extension of my own life force. As they grew, I arranged them all around me, creating a protective circle. My brain and the cerebrochip's firewall were now interfacing perfectly.

My efforts, however, did not go undetected and I felt my father's anger flood into me. A psychic shock wave hacked through my universe, threatening to tear me to pieces.

I willed the spheres into motion. It proved harder than it had been during my visualisation training, and I could feel the fear threatening to overtake me. I ignored it and focused on shaping the sphere's trajectories, arcing their paths so each one revolved around me in a specific orbit. Once I had accomplished this I commanded them to ever faster speeds, generating a defensive shell about me.

Yet as powerful as my shield was, I could still sense the fingers of my father's consciousness burrowing through.

"Ah, a fighter to the end, Alex," his voice echoed as he negotiated his way through the barriers. "I'll enjoy your body that much more."

The shield I had erected was not strong enough to stop him, but that was part of the trap.

He began to break through and in this strange, virtual universe he resembled an elongated, ashen corpse. Bulbous red eyes stared at me and a black swollen tongue slicked over daggered teeth as he twisted his hideous form towards me. Yet each movement served to entangle him more and more with the energy shells.

He stretched out a taloned hand. "Nowhere to run Alex," the skeletal face sneered. "Nowhere to go."

"I'm not trying to run," I told him. "Take a look—you're trapped." I snatched hold of his bony wrist before the talons could pierce my neck.

"It's over, you evil son of a bitch," I said. "You're not the spider anymore. You're the fly."

I let control of the shield go and concentrated my whole being on exploding it outwards. The stick-like frame of my father, interlinked with the shield, shredded into fragments as the energy shells continued to expand at greater and greater velocities. His screams filled the void and some part of me still connected to him shared his agony.

I watched as the splintered strips of energy faded into the distance and realised I was entirely alone. For a moment I feared I might be imprisoned inside this virtual limbo, but then reminded myself that I was master here now. I willed the darkness away and it retreated.

I reopened my eyes and saw the strobes above me dim whilst the metal claws flailed in their death throes.

I suddenly felt intensely claustrophobic, like I'd been buried alive. I yanked the cilia from the back of my skull and slammed my hands against the casket lid. It slid back and I sat up, gulping in cool, oxygen-rich air.

As I crawled out of what was meant to be my tomb, I saw an army of insectoid machines waiting. Sian stood paralyzed in the middle of them, too frightened to move. Yet none of the things showed any activity and I noticed that their optical circuits were non-operational. The old man must have linked everything up to his own consciousness. When his mind had ceased, his creations, devoid of a master, did too.

I turned and noticed Talbot standing beside me.

He gave a small bow.

"All went well I trust, sir," he said.

I nodded. "As planned."

The servant was silent for some moments. "I monitored some anomalies during the transfer," he went on, regarding me closely.

"The host was more resistant than expected," I replied. I stepped down from the raised platform and surveyed the room anxiously. My father was a cautious man and never took anything for granted. It wouldn't be this easy.

I wasn't disappointed. A few seconds later, a trio of glass canisters poked from the walls and a one-minute countdown flashed up on the screen behind me. I studied the sulphurous gas undulating inside the canisters and guessed it was some kind of nerve toxin set to be released.

The countdown began.

"The password, sir," Talbot said, "if you please."

The old man, it seemed, intended to make sure that if he perished then so would I. But something had happened within that virtual world that he hadn't bargained for.

Although my father's ego had been destroyed, many of his thought patterns had nevertheless been imprinted on mine during the attempted transfer. I could almost still feel his presence.

I shut my eyes and sifted through the remnants of his mind in my own. Images streamed through my head until a single word materialized: "Lazarus."

A fitting password for someone wishing to cheat death.

I spoke the word aloud and the countdown terminated at eighteen seconds. The canisters retracted once more into the walls.

"Welcome back, sir," Talbot said.

It took me a couple of days and a sleepless night to hook the entire residence up to my own ECG patterns and place everything under my direct will. I spent another half-day re-programming Talbot. The android was just too dangerous to leave as he was—who knew what other fail-safes the old man had programmed into him. Finally, I'd dealt with the lawyers who had officially declared me sole legal heir.

There was only one other loose end to tie up now.

A woman's footsteps patted up behind me.

"You asked to see me?" Sian said.

I didn't turn to face her, but rather continued to gaze down at the sprawling earth-bound city below and the wisps of clouds that obscured much of it. I was beginning to understand how the inhabitants up here had come to think of themselves as gods.

"How do you like living up here?" I asked her.

"It's paradise," she answered, a tinge of nervousness in her voice.

"Good, because you're married to a very powerful man now. I've set the whole west wing aside for you, and Talbot will arrange memberships to all the best clubs. I recommend the tennis club, it's the most exclusive."

I clasped my hands behind my back.

"Now, if you don't mind, I have matters to attend to. When I need you I will send for you."

I sensed her confusion, her eyes staring perplexedly at my back, then heard her turn and go. I glanced over my shoulder after a moment, just before she reached the elevator. I noticed the contented swagger in her walk.

I expelled a contented sigh of my own. I'd won. I'd taken on one of the most powerful men on Eden and won.

It was time to contemplate my future. I had been a rich man before, but now I could use my spectacular wealth to really help humanity, to be a benefactor to all. The sense of power that imbued me felt very gratifying. Yet as I dwelt on the subject I found I no longer cared.

To hell with my fellow man.

I had a new destiny. I was now in a position to become the most formidable figure Eden had ever seen. And I alone could gain control over the ant colony I viewed below me. Who could challenge me?

I took a deep, bracing breath of cold air and let out a laugh. It was then I realised the voice was no longer my own.

Time to Find Charley

Catherine Edmunds

The gates are locked. Sophia can see no way around or over them as they're topped with coils of razor wire. Someone has stuck incongruous bunches of dead weeds and flower heads through the bars, presumably to pretty them up, or maybe to commemorate the dead.

The gates might not be as strong as they look. Sophia closes her fingers around a bar next to the force field protected lock, ignoring the splinters of rust that scrape her palm. She pulls. The gates creak but refuse to budge. She tries another bar, tugging harder. The hinges groan in protest but shrug off her feeble attempt.

She walks away, disconsolate, and sits on a pile of discarded laser blasters facing a tree stump. There is something familiar about this scene and she's determined to understand its significance.

A man's head, white-haired and wrinkled—such an ugly thing—perches on the surface of the stump. Sophia picks up a blaster and throws it at the head. She misses. Of course she bloody misses. She was never any good at marksmanship at the academy. She picks up another, much heavier one and chucks it. The blaster falls short by meter or so.

You throw like a girl.

Bloody don't.

She marches to the stump, snatches up the blaster, and smashes it down upon the head. It shatters, sending splashes of brain and shards of skull in all directions. Globs of mucus land on her overalls, adding to the dried stains already there. She ignores them. It's time she found Charley. If she can't force her way through the gates, she'll go a different route. She turns away, dismissing the scene from her mind, and walks down the filthy walkways towards the spaceport.

He's here. Sophia can see him through the plexiglass window looking at a hologram. An image of a woman, she thinks, but it's difficult to be certain as the view is obscured by hieroglyphs scratched onto the pane. The pale scribbles resemble battleships from a distance, but now that she is closer, she can make out words—poems?—about eating and food and hunger. About thirst.

She goes inside and inserts coins into a food vend. The coffee in the cracked beaker trembles, sending ripples back and forth in concentric circles. The bitter aroma nauseates her and she puts it down in disgust. A few faded pages of diagrams from an engineering manual lie stained with blood on a table. She can smell air freshener—cut pine. It turns her stomach. She can't stay here.

She hurries back to the gates, but the graffiti on the smouldering walls stings her out of her resolve. It's so cold. Incredibly cold. Icicles of bereavement shriek through the night and sever all hope. She yanks up a handful of weeds and sticks them through the railings, trying to remember why. Rusting iron drips a stream of malignancy. She follows its course away from the gates and across the river, thick with sulphurous sludge. Nameless pieces of flesh float by. Black slime oozes out of distended walls and barred doors gurgle soft and low.

Another window, brightly lit. She thinks she can see her own image, like an oil painting, taunting her. Summertime, hands folded across a muslin gown, strings of pearls, a smile that bodes ill. The picture hangs by a thread, its wire support frayed and insistent, demanding she remember how to fall.

There he is.

There's Charley. It's really him this time, huddled in a gutter. She recognises his threadbare coat with its worn cuffs.

"Hey, Charley," she says. "I know where we can find you something to eat. Something clean. Safe. Fresh water."

Charley's once lustrous hair, now white and desperate, moves in the hot breeze blowing from the overhead vent. Sophia thinks she sees glowworms, but it's just a trick of the phosphorescent lighting. She stretches out her hand.

He lifts his face to her and speaks with a voice full of gravel and dread.

"I can't."

Fear crawls around his neck and tightens.

"Food," says Sophia. "C'mon."

Charley rises unsteadily to his feet.

A mechanical millipede drops out of his right sleeve and scuttles towards a drain. Sophia steps on it with a crunch, then stoops down and scoops it up.

"Food," she says once again and stuffs the creature into Charley's mouth.

He swallows and gags.

Sophia seizes his lapels and shoves him against the wall. He smells of despair, and for a moment she almost pities him until she remembers he's an ugly thing, with his silvery white hair. And she has a knife.

Later, a pile of rags lies on the floor, twisted together like so many limbs torn from their bodies, wrapped in winding sheets and left to rot. A swarm of black flies descends. The bundle of rags wriggles. Alive maybe? No, impossible, but the ground is fractured and desiccated and bleeds misery into the river. Christ in a dressing gown carries a plastic cross. A trick of the light makes it appear as if one of his legs ends in a cloven hoof. Radioactive paint trickles from his brow where a crown of thorny twigs attempts to signal danger and pain. A black crow enfolds its wings around his neck to give him warmth and succour.

Down at the spaceport, a giant structure of rust allows a little light to penetrate, dissipating the shades of travellers who were here before. The river runs sluggishly, feeding the dreams of white cabin-pods which sink in the mud and sup each night when the tides of light come in.

Dawn breaks over the dome. A row of three damaged starcruisers catches the sun, the low beams showing their ruptured sides more clearly than is wise. Secrets are hidden here, but the tall buildings soon send their extrusions to hide any hints of salvation.

Sophia awakens, sees hypos and foil. Mouldering leaves, broken glass, a piece of metal whetted like a knife, designed to pass through any security system. Torn cuffs on the sleeves of a coat. She remembers the cuffs.

"Charley? Charley! Listen to me!"

"No," he replies. "Just leave me be. I won't go to the city. We've discussed this before."

"We have to go. The water here is toxic, we can't drink it. We'll die of thirst if we stay. Is that what you want? Is that to be the sum of your life? A parched, swollen throat and a slow agonising death because you're too proud to seek out an alternative?"

"Better dead, believe me. You want to be one of them? Better dead, truly dead."

"You're wrong, Charley. Anything is preferable to that sort of finality. In the city they walk. They have animation of some sort. That's hope, surely? Isn't it?"

Sophia can just see Charley in the dawn's dim ascent. His eyes are shut and his body curled up. Death sits in the ditch beside him, cradling an axe.

She makes one last attempt.

"Charley, I can't stay here. I have to survive. The city is only a short walk away. We're not far from the gates."

He rouses himself to speak.

"Then go. Walk into that accursed place. But you walk alone. I stay here to live out the last few moments of my life as I choose."

"Moments? Charley please!"

Frustrated, she picks up a junked laser blaster and flings it. Misses.

"You throw like a girl!"

He chuckles, and she can't bear it.

And then, movement. A shadow. A breath on her cheek and a laugh in the dark. A waiting presence, taking substance, smelling of decay. Rotting meat. And though her soul cries out for sustenance, she knows she must never drink from this source. The knowledge comes too late. She hears the percussive sound of an explosion in the distance, then a creak and a faint green glow as something fissures overhead.

"Charley, there are worse things here than you can know. Come with me. Please."

There's no reply. A fog, a dull green miasma, seeps into the gutter, taking form. No time to think, must act.

A piece of metal, whetted like a knife. A cry, like a benediction. Something sticky.

Sophia clambers out of the gutter and lurches toward the city. Her footsteps leave permanent shadows on the ground, but she never looks back, never knows she's trailing flakes of leprous flesh.

The gates are barred. Locked. Razor wire draped in haphazard coils around bent spikes. Someone has pushed dead weeds through the bars. Sophia closes her two remaining fingers around the padlock and pulls. The hinges groan in protest but shrug off her feeble attempt.

There's a tree stump. A man's head. It's an ugly thing.

You throw like a girl!

Bloody don't.

She smashes a laser blaster down on the head, grabs handfuls of brains, slurps them down through her toothless gums and vomits up gobbets of putrescence.

Time to find Charley.

Mesozoic Appetite

Thomas Kleaton

Ed Flann imagined the taste of French toast made with dinosaur eggs.

He had known something was amiss with his chickens the second he opened the henhouse door. Warm fingers of late afternoon sunlight slanted in, illuminating the floor in the shape of the doorframe. Pine shavings from the nesting boxes fluttered around as several Rhode Island Reds chased a Barred Rock around the floor, pecking at its back.

Ed reached up and tugged the pull chain of the single naked bulb hanging by a cord.

The hens scattered into the shadows as light flooded the room. He caught a glimpse of Armin, his American Game rooster, springing off the roost. It soared toward him, wings flapping, and its claws plowed his cheek on the way down, leaving deep red grooves.

"Son-of-a-bitch!" Ed said, wiping his face with his work glove. Blood streaked the fingertips.

You know Horace will be hitting on Irma, don't you?

Miss Pully, his prize white Leghorn, was talking to him again. It seemed she spoke to him a lot lately.

They've both been snickering behind your back. He just can't wait to slip his dirty hands into her panties. And Alfred, that wily rascal, always scheming ways to buy your farm out from under you. Where will you live then, Ed? I suppose there are a few rooms available in the old folks home.

"Shut up! Shut up! Shut up!" Ed's hands shot to his ears to stifle her idle chatter. He then grasped her by the wings, laying her off to the side of the nest to retrieve her eggs. Squawking loudly, she nipped at his arm. A sharp pain jolted him. Ed knew Leghorns aggressively defended their eggs, but Miss Pully had never *attacked* him.

"What's wrong with you, girl?"

Ed rubbed the stinging welt on his arm. An array of pin-pricks dimpled his leathery skin, oozing red. He studied Miss Pully's keen beak through his Coke-bottle glasses.

Teeth, he realized.

This hen's got teeth!

Several rows of tiny, serrated incisors bristled from her mandibles. He palmed her yellow claws in his glove. They were thicker, longer than a common hen's, curving into fine points resembling more the killing talons of a hawk than the scratching nails of a chicken.

He turned to Armin, who was observing him from his roost. Closer inspection showed that he too was cutting teeth, as were the other hens.

Ed's fingers went absentmindedly to his cheek, caressing the wounds. He set Miss Pully back into the nesting box. She clucked at him and raised her wings, indignant, while he gathered her speckled white eggs into the basket he carried. He removed his sweaty "World's Greatest Pig Farmer" cap and scratched his head, puzzled by his hens' new physical attributes.

Maybe she's a mutant, he supposed.

Ed jotted a mental note to check on her frequently. Check on all of them. He was a man who liked to take good care of his laying hens.

Ed stepped into the kitchen, fragrant with the smell of cooking pot roast, just as his wife Irma was hanging up the phone.

Probably talking dirty to Horace.

"Don't forget, dear, Uncle Horace is coming over on Sunday," said Irma. She was preparing the mashed potatoes, cutting them up and dropping them in chunks into a pot of simmering water. A Ziploc freezer bag of frozen field peas sat thawing on the counter.

"And you know how Uncle Horace just loves grilled chicken."

Ed grumbled under his breath. The very thought of Irma being around Horace had him seething.

He tried to banish it from his mind by watching TV in the den. He plopped down onto his recliner, the soft suede coddling his aching back. The pout on his face eased into a slight smile as one of his favorite shows, *Jurassic Fight Club*, came on the History Channel. A Tyrannosaurus rex had a Nanotyrannus gripped in its jagged teeth when Irma hollered from the kitchen.

"Dinner time!"

He ignored her for a minute before tapping the power button on the remote.

"Don't make me call you again, Ed Flann," she said while wiping the countertop with a damp dishrag.

"All right, I'm coming," he replied, rising. "Can't a man relax around here?"

He parked himself in one of the wooden chairs at the table, wincing as its rungs dug into his spine. Ice tinkled in his glass as Irma poured sweet tea into it. He waited until she filled her plate, then seized a substantial slab of pot roast so quickly it slid off the serving fork and landed half-on, half-off his plate.

"Don't be so greedy, Ed," she said, her brows creasing in disapproval. "If you make a mess you'll be eating slop from the trough with the rest of your pigs."

"Who else is coming over Sunday? Not Alfred and Joyce, are they?"

"You know who's coming," said Irma as she peppered her mashed potatoes. "We discussed this last month. Uncle Horace will be here, and so will Joyce and Alfred."

Alfred, Irma's older brother, and Ed did not get along well. Ed was primarily a pig farmer, his two hundred pigs divided by paddocks on five acres of their ten-acre property. Their house sat on the other five acres, along with the henhouse and a sizable plot where Ed grew his corn. Alfred was an investment banker, always hounding Ed to sell his farm to him and move Irma to a residence in the suburbs where life would be easier on her. But he suspected Alfred's motives ran much deeper. New industries were pouring into Baldwin County, and companies needed land to build factories.

Alfred also had an annoying habit of taking out his false teeth at the table, something Ed just couldn't stomach.

"I hate the thought of grilling chicken for Horace," said Ed. "He'll be wanting to take all the leftovers home."

"Simmer down, sweetie. It's just Sunday dinner."

Ed, drowsy from overstuffing himself, dozed off in his recliner after dinner and dreamed of dinosaurs mating with chickens.

The next morning, Irma was up early, cooking breakfast. The aromas of frying bacon and brewing coffee pervaded their home. Ed gulped down his meal, then headed out the door. It was mid October, and his lungs filled with the crisp, cool air as he gazed at the lush corn glittering with dew. A crow cawed somewhere off in the field, hidden by the tall stalks. It was almost harvest time.

Armin screeched at him through the wire of the chicken run. Ed crossed over to the henhouse, peeping in cautiously as he sidled through the door.

Pandemonium greeted his eyes. Of his fourteen laying hens, only two were nesting. The others skittered around the small space, nipping at one another. Ed's initial thought was that a vicious free-for-all had taken place in the coop.

Talk about pecking order! Miss Pully twittered at him.

He examined her first, holding her by the wings. White feathers fell out by the dozens as he lifted her. Her claws were stretched, spiky. She hooked them into his arm, trying to gain purchase in her attempt to roost on his cap. He dropped her back into the nesting box, where she bared her new teeth at him and made short clicking sounds.

You remember, don't you, Ed? she said, her yellow eyes locked on Ed's. *The weekend at the motel while you were out of town at the farmers conference? The weekend you weren't supposed to know about?*

"Shut up!" Ed barked.

The weekend she'd gone to him out of pity, the weekend Horace rode her the way your hog, Beezer, rides your sows.

Irma had come to Ed tearfully afterwards, unable to bear the awesome weight of her guilt, confessing their little tryst. He'd forgiven her, but distrust had rooted and bloomed into a particularly ugly blossom.

Ed peered at Miss Pully's skull. It was definitely larger, as was the beak. He again inspected the teeth. They were at least a quarter-inch long now, resembling the sharp canines of dogs. The silky feathers on top of her head were molting, the exposed skin looking like smooth pebbles in a streambed. The eyes were the worst, her pupils shrunken into tiny black dots, appraising him like a snake staring down a rat. As he petted the top of her head, her comb peeled off on his glove, like a dying rose petal, withered and black.

Ed stood there, musing about a recent TV show he had seen—*Dinosaurs: Return to Life?*—where scientists discussed how birds and chickens had once had teeth and arms instead of wings, about transcription factors and atavisms. They had talked about reactivating dormant genes. Ed recalled news stories about birds sprouting tails with vertebrae and extra fins appearing on fish.

Genes.

If they can be turned off, surely they can be turned back on?

He suspected this was what was happening to his hens.

Maybe it's the feed, he thought. Maybe some ingredient is affecting his chickens. Or the chickens that'd spawned his chickens. Ed read about such things in his farm journals. Shit being added to feather meal, like antibiotics, acetaminophen, and arsenic.

While stroking Miss Pully, he probed her wing feathers as gently as his gloved hand would allow, as if searching for fleas. There, growing from the jaundiced skin at each of her wing tips, he spotted a dwarf chicken claw comprised of two gnarled digits.

Ed dashed backwards out the door, shutting and locking it as Armin strutted toward him unleashing a volley of clucks, his teeth threatening.

Late Saturday afternoon arrived too soon for Ed. Irma was away at the local Kroger supermarket, shopping for their weekly supplies. She hoped to find a Mrs. Smith's pie for Alfred, apple being his favorite, although she knew it gave him the backyard trots.

Ed looked intently through the window at the thin slice of chicken run visible from the kitchen. Gray steel mesh on rough timber silhouetted against the darkening azure sky, mimicking prison fencing. All that was needed to complete the scenario was looping razor wire.

Not a bad idea, Ed thought.

The sink was half-full of cold water, ready to scrub the chickens in. He shut off the spigot and pulled a hefty meat cleaver from one of the drawers. Donning his heaviest work gloves, he clutched the cleaver firmly and then plodded out toward the henhouse on his grim task, letting the screen door bang shut behind him.

So old Horace wants grilled chicken, huh? Wait 'til he gets a taste of this!

Ed stopped, ear cocked toward the henhouse.

Scratching sounds, like a dog clawing at wood, echoed through the walls. He swallowed, then directed his eyes skyward at the pale crust of the moon. Whistling to himself, he traced the faint outline of the Cassiopeia constellation with his finger.

He took more tentative steps and paused at the henhouse door, listening, then unfastened it and stepped inside.

The smell was ghastly, like dead rats drowned in uneaten slop rotting in a pig trough in the blistering heat of the sun. Fuzzy half-light permeated the henhouse, and the scratching was now intermingled with dull rapping vibrations, like a woodpecker boring into a pecan tree.

Ed shuffled forward into the shadows, spotting a hairless, loathsome tail jutting from under the lower nesting boxes.

Possum.

He stamped his boot onto the tail. Armin trumpeted in pain and squirmed out from beneath his hiding place. He scurried across the floor and vaulted through the small wall opening leading into the chicken run beyond. The automatic chicken door, activated by its timer, slid silently down on oiled tracks.

Ed, startled, yanked the pull chain of the overhead light, shadows shifting as the lit bulb swung back and forth.

A bevy of vultures dining on road kill flashed through his mind, and he stifled the urge to vomit. A lengthy gore-encrusted skeleton lay semi-coiled over the floorboards, the pitiful remains of a chicken snake that had slithered in. Black ants crawled in and out of its mouth, and the creatures that now only scarcely resembled his hens were busily scarfing up what tattered tidbits of flesh they could without incurring the pecks of their sisters. Their feathers flaked off like seedpods from a dandelion. Their hides were animated with tiny scales instead of feathers, mimicking the festering skin of the reptile they were feasting on rather than a plucked fowl.

Ed, scowling, noticed his hens were displaying rat-like tails as well.

Then, a movement in his peripheral vision. One of the hens, half-concealed in pine shavings on the upmost shelf, leaped onto his shoulder with a shrill cry, digging its talons into the side of his neck. The toothy beak gaped and clamped down on his eyebrow, while its bare-bones right wing folded forward, the two razor-sharp claws at the end raking at his eyeball.

Ed collapsed, having tripped over another hen running in circles between his feet like a scrappy little dog. The cleaver fell from his hand and clattered onto the floor.

Snatching the hen from his shoulder by the scruff, he flung the chicken around him and cracked it like a whip, fracturing its neck. It sagged in his grip and he tossed it aside.

He could hear Armin outside, snapping his jaws like an agitated gator.

Ed scrabbled for the cleaver and picked it up. The heaviness of it felt *right* in his hand. He sat up, blood coursing over his eye in a red haze.

He saw the other birds scuttling toward him, a herd of avian imps attracted by the coppery odor. He struggled to his knees, mopping his eye with his shirtsleeve, then to his feet. He brandished the meat cleaver over his head, imitating a Civil War cavalry officer raising his sword in battle, and fled the coop.

Okay, Ed realized. I'm gonna need one more fryer.

Irma returned home just after seven p.m., plunking sacks of groceries onto the kitchen countertop.

"I'm sorry I'm so late, dear. Kroger had a really good sale going on," she said, pulling cans of butterbeans from a bag. "I had to find an apple pie for Albert, and potatoes for Uncle Horace. I'm making a gigantic bowl of potato salad. He'll be wanting seconds, I'm sure."

And thirds and fourths, Ed thought.

Irma placed the milk in the refrigerator, spying the pans of cut-up chicken sitting in chilled water on the second shelf.

"Good. I see you've already prepared the chicken. Are you going to make some of your special barbecue sauce for Uncle Horace?"

Of course, Irma. Just tell me what kind of sauce goes with tyrannosaur meat. Crushed ginkgo nuts cooked in birch sap? Deadly nightshade?

"Sure," Ed replied. "If I can find the Tabasco sauce."

"I hope frozen pizza's okay with you. It's a little late to be cooking anything. I'll be doing enough of *that* tomorrow."

Irma started preheating the oven and stuck Alfred's pie in the freezer. Then she noticed the scabbed ridge on Ed's eyebrow.

"What happened to your eye, Ed?"

"Got too close to some chicken wire," he answered.

Albert and Joyce drove up promptly at 5:30 p.m. Sunday afternoon.

Joyce wore beige khakis and a pretty sapphire cardigan over a simple white camisole. Albert was dressed more casual in a white button-up shirt and blue jeans.

"Hi, sis! Is that apple pie I smell?" he said, hugging Irma.

"It sure is, Beets," Irma replied. She'd called her brother Beets since they were children, when their mother caught him with a lapful of them he had ripped from her vegetable garden. "I know how you love apple pie!

"Where's Ed?"

"He's outside grilling chicken."

Albert wrinkled his nose.

"Oh, don't frown up like that! I'm also baking a meat-loaf."

"Do you need any help in the kitchen, Irma?" asked Joyce.

"Well, I could use a hand with the potato salad," she said. "And we can chitchat about how my favorite niece is doing in college."

Joyce was stirring the potato salad in a stainless steel bowl and Irma wrapping the warm pie in aluminum foil when the doorbell chimed.

"I'll get it," said Albert, rising from his chair.

"Howdy, Albert!" boomed Uncle Horace at the doorstep. He stood about 5' 11" tall, with a massive waistline. He was almost completely bald, and wore black horn-rimmed eyeglasses, the type popularized during the heyday of singer Buddy Holly. His breath reeked of whiskey.

"Come in, Uncle Horace."

Horace was Irma's uncle by marriage. Aunt Ruby, her mother's youngest sister, wasn't much older than Irma, and they grew up together like siblings. She had passed away of congestive heart failure only eighteen months before. Horace, nine years older than Ruby, had arrived sloshed for his wife's funeral. Ed found out later that Horace propositioned Irma right there in the chapel. "He was drunk," Irma had said. "And grieving. Let bygones be bygones, Ed."

Ed wished Horace *was* gone.

"Hello, Irma," said Horace, waddling into the kitchen. He had just turned seventy, and looked to weigh about two-hundred-eighty pounds. He reached into a drawer and seized a fork, jammed it into the bowl of potato salad, and shoveled a tremendous piece of spud into his mouth.

"You stop that right now, Uncle Horace. We're about to eat!" Irma's brow was furrowed, her lips pursed.

Horace brayed with laughter, spitting bits of potato onto the linoleum floor.

The screen door squeaked, and Ed waltzed in carrying a platter of grilled chicken. He set it down on the counter, glowering at Horace, whose beady eyes were brazenly tracing the curvature of Irma's cleavage.

Ed saw Miss Pully atop the refrigerator, admonishing him with her piercing stare. He clenched his eyelids shut a moment until his torment waned. When he reopened them, the freakish, faulting hen was no longer there.

"You okay, Eddie?" Horace asked.

Ed nodded and smiled, a smile as cold as the milk Joyce was now mixing into the potato salad.

"Ahh, great dinner, sis," said Alfred. "How about a slice of that pie now?"

He was polishing off his meatloaf and washing it down with iced tea. The women gorged themselves on the potato salad and butterbeans. Only Horace had touched the grilled chicken. From the corner of his eye Ed watched as he'd taken his first hearty bite, juices flowing down his chin. He was now chomping into a plump thigh with those horse-like teeth of his.

"On second thought, Irma, I think I'll take it home with me," Alfred said. "We've got to be up early in the morning."

He flipped his upper denture out of his mouth, balancing it on his tongue. Ed cringed.

"You know, Eddie, this is some fine chicken," Horace said through a mouthful of meat. "Almost as fine as li'l Irma here."

Ed's forehead scrunched and the tips of his ears glowed red. He watched Irma. Her eyes were focused on Horace, her lips partially parted. She was giving him that *look*. The same look she had once given Ed, when he was still able to love her the way she yearned to be loved.

"If you don't mind," continued Horace, "I'd like to take a few pieces home with me. And a few scoops of that potato salad too." He was ogling Irma's chest. *Again.*

"I've got an idea, Horace," Ed said, clapping him on the shoulder. "Why don't you come out to the henhouse with me? Grab a couple of those empty egg cartons by the door and get yourself a couple dozen fresh eggs to bring home with you as well!"

Horace's eyes lit up.

"I think I'll take you up on that, Eddie."

Horace's chair scraped the floor as he shifted it away from the table. Irma switched on the porch lamp while Ed led him out into the yard.

A manure-perfumed breeze accompanied them as they traversed the distance to the henhouse. Ed unlatched the door and cracked it open.

"Just slide on in there, Horace. There's a light hanging in the middle of the room with a pull chain. You can't miss it."

Horace stumbled into the dark, the egg cartons dangling from his fingertips.

"So you like to gawk at breasts, do ya? Get a load of *these*, you son-of-a-bitch!"

Ed shoved Horace inside, slamming the door shut behind him and securing the bolt.

"Let me out, you asshole!" Horace bawled.

Ed heard Horace jerk the pull chain. He saw a flurry of shadows dancing in the light. A crescendo of screeches and yowls shattered the night. Ed could hear Armin shrieking. A horrible wail rose above the din. Blows rained down on the wood.

Splashes of blood. A cloud of feathers.

Ed never flinched.

The three of them stood on the porch, Joyce shivering in the frosty air.

"Well, we really do have to be going, sis," said Alfred. "But we enjoyed ourselves. And thanks for the pie!"

"I have no clue what's keeping them so long," Irma said. "Ed!" she shouted toward the henhouse. "Horace! Don't you make me come fetch you two!"

Alfred's throat constricted when he spotted Ed stepping into the feeble light cast by the porch lamp. He was gazing upward, calm, surveying the night sky. He staggered forward a mite further, then halted.

Irma's eyes widened. "Oh dear, you're hurt!"

Wet crimson spattered Ed's overalls; his face was daubed with war paint from his blood-dipped fingers. One glimpse into his sunken eye sockets told them Ed's mind had gone someplace else. Someplace bad.

"Ed, what have you done?" Irma gaped at his hand. Joyce gasped.

Confused, he looked down, hardly registering the cleaver he held, or the ruby stickiness that smeared its blade.

"Miss Pully's upset," Ed muttered. "She just hasn't been herself lately. And Armin…"

Alfred raced across the yard to the henhouse and gagged at the sight of all the bodies, of Horace and the chickens soaked in gore, hacked up beyond recognition.

"Joyce, you and Al gotta come over for dinner next week," Ed said with a deranged smile. "We're having *ribs!*"

Pet

Sawney Hatton

"Every living thing requires something on which to feed in order to live. A pet depends on its master to feed it; therefore it is the master's burden—at its most fundamental—to maintain the pet's life."

Jusita Lu Yeffar, COO
Mhurian Empathy for Organism Welfare
(MEOW) Int'g

Pinky's master is Stacia Moz, perhaps the brightest and positively the prettiest roprogrammer at the Gamma-One Automaton Designworks. She has natural blonde curls, double-dimpled cheeks, and the beautiful ovoid eyes characteristic of native-born Pyzureks. And her body, flawless by all current standards in the Mhuri Galaxy.

Stacia is, as they say, *hot as Hoggra!*

Her boyfriend Dex ranks only a Level C-5 Engineer in the Exo-Skeleton Department—he failed the C-4 certification twice—but he is handsome, charming, and devoted. Good enough for Stacia, most of their fellow plant workers agree.

(And even those who don't can understand the attraction.) By all appearances they are a well-matched couple.

Stacia and Dex had met in the south wing commissary at lunch during the summer. He accidentally spilled her jollup juice. Not only did he buy her another cup, but also a cocoanut pudding, which she shared with him.

By autumn, they'd moved in together into a luxury skyrise apartment in downtown Trivicon City. He made her breakfast every day, and she made love to him every night.

They were happy then.

Stacia was never allowed any pets growing up at her parents' home on Nabaru, because her papi didn't ever think she was responsible enough, and her mums was allergic to near about everything anyway. Stacia had told Dex again and again how she'd always wanted a pet of her own. He got the hint.

Dex bought the creature from an interplanetary trading freighter and brought it home as a birthday gift for Stacia. Commonly called a fluffox (its zoological name is ridiculously long to spell and near impossible to pronounce), they are popular companion animals among the upper castes, prized for both their docility and cuteness.

A fluffox most resembles the brindle-fleeced head of a male Wixian lion, minus the snout. Its eyes are large, round, and rheumy—adorable sad puppy eyes. Lacking the prototypical mammalian mouth, it can only ingest liquid nutrients through the hairless, sea anemone-like stalk protruding from its shaggy face. It also has bird-like feet, and bald rosy-hued hindquarters much like the baboons of Earth. For this reason Stacia named it Pinky.

Stacia plays games of fetch with Pinky and its vulcanized toys whenever she has the spare moment. She takes it out for short conveyor walks, cleans up after it, scolds it when it misbehaves. And she feeds it, mostly scrowz milk, but occasionally treats it to snow viper broth if she remembers to pick up a carton from the market.

In contrast to Stacia, Dex is not much of an animal person. He has never really liked Pinky. But he likes how much Stacia seems to like it. That's enough for him.

For a while it was anyway. Dex scarcely bends a finger to help care for the creature. *It's your damn fluffox*, he tells Stacia. *It's your job to take care of it.*

Taking care of Pinky eventually becomes a taxing chore for Stacia. It constantly grovels for food and whines for attention. It knocks things over, messes the floors, wakes her up in the middle of the night.

Some of Stacia and Dex's coworkers believe this was the spark that had lit the fuse to what ultimately detonated their relationship.

But most think Stacia was just too good for him. They could never last.

Nobody is quite sure when his boozing began, but a year after Stacia had settled down with him, Dex was terminated from the Gamma-One plant. He had a tough time finding alternate work and soon gave up trying. Instead he aimed to drink himself every day to the brink of insensibility, until he could feel nothing anymore.

Nothing but anger.

Dex often comes home battered and bruised from starting fights at the local saloons with whoever happened to provoke him that evening for whatever reason.

He raises his fists to Stacia if she nags him about it. Or if she tries to calm him down. Or if he just has the urge to strike something.

One day Stacia decides to break it off with Dex. She no longer loves him, she tells him as the transporters haul her stuff from the apartment. She is fed up with his raging and rampaging. He's unambitious and lazy and worthless. She doesn't see a future with him.

Dex begs for her to stay. Promises he'll change. Yells she'll regret dumping him. Smashes a full bottle of ninety proof Krevvar against the wall.

Unswayed by his pleas, Stacia departs Dex's life.

And leaves poor Pinky behind with him.

Three days later, Dex staggers over to Stacia's new place of residence. He's learned she has become romantically involved with Mr. Bogg'ins, the Vice President of Sales at Gamma-One, and now shares his uptown manorplex.

Dex bangs on the door. Bawling, he asks her to forgive him, to please come back, to give them another chance.

Mr. Bogg'ins calls the constables on him.

I need you Stacia, Dex sobs as they escort him, wrists shackled, into the raptech cruiser. From the backseat he looks out at the expensive home, his eyes ricocheting from one window to another. He never sees her.

A night in the drunk cell humbles Dex.

From then on, when all the saloons have closed for the day and he returns to his lonely home and crawls into his empty bed, all Dex craves before drifting off to a fitful sleep is to hurt something as badly as Stacia hurt him.

Pinky naps in its corner by the photon stove. Dex sits at the kitchenette table, finishing off a Quilq eight-pack. He glares at the fluffox flopped on his floor. He is already sick and tired of filling its feeder and wiping up its muddy poop.

Yet it is the last thing he has that connects him to Stacia.

Oh how he misses her.

Now that she's gone, maybe it's best to get rid of the hairy beast. Go ditch it on the crossway. Let it fend for itself. Or get whacked by a jetbus. Whatever.

Dex rises from his chair and looms over Pinky. He sets the sole of his foot on the creature's head and slowly applies pressure. Pinky's big eyes widen, then wince. It scratches at Dex's chaffan pants and squirms its plump body, struggling to wriggle out from under his djarvian leather boot. Dex pushes down harder. The creature is trapped there, at his mercy. He wants to crush it. He wants to see its brains burst from its skull.

But when Pinky whimpers pitifully, Dex lifts his foot. It scurries away, cowers beneath the kitchenette table.

Dex lights a cigarella and tries to think about nothing.

The next night, Dex arrives home earlier than usual—though still much later than most people who work regular daily shifts—his nose busted and his bottom lip split from another brawl. He slams his door shut upon entering.

Pinky, sniffing at a dead myl beetle, swivels toward Dex, alarmed.

Dex kicks the creature, launching it across the room. It hits the bookcase, bouncing off and rolling halfway over the parlor rug. It scampers into the bedroom, hides beneath his bed.

Dex laughs, licking his bloodied lip.

The following morning, Dex chases Pinky throughout the apartment, gleefully flinging knives and tines at it. It darts under his bed again, panting and trembling.

Dex flips on the Tel3V and plops into his lounger to catch the end of *The Greco Granite Show.*

Dex has not fed Pinky for a week now. While he is out at the saloons, it digs through the kitchenette waste bin for any rotting food soft enough to consume. It also learns to suck up the green mold growing along the baseboards.

Twice a day, if he remembers, Dex leashes the creature on the balcony where it can do its business. Often he leaves it out there for hours, even in the rain, until it whines and howls and scratches at the sliding window. Once he gets annoyed enough, Dex will let it back inside.

Pinky always runs away from him.

On Wednesday or Thursday (what does it matter anymore?) Dex brings home a bag of cheap Oongolese food. He sits down at the kitchenette table, eating from the styroweave containers.

Pinky observes him intensely, its stalk wagging, saliva dripping from the tip. Dex, enjoying his meal, ignores it.

The creature pounces onto the table and overturns a box of biomac stew. It spatters onto the floor. Pinky leaps down and siphons the gravy greedily.

Dex smashes his fist down on its spine. Pinky grunts, then whips its stalk out and snatches the barbecue woplings from the tabletop. Dex attempts to grab them from it, but Pinky honks at him and dashes underneath the bed, slurping up the sauce, watching him with wary eyes.

Frik you too, Dex grumbles.

Another day. After going through a pack of Quilq ale and a book of cigarellas, Dex rises to use the lav.

He discovers Pinky perched on the toilet rim, drinking from the basin.

With the palm of his hand, Dex shoves the creature down into the water. He holds it under the surface until the air bubbles taper off. He then yanks it up and hurls it into the shower pod beside him.

Pinky gasps for breath as Dex relieves himself. Grinning, he blows cigarella smoke in its face.

Dex is almost out of funds on his savings stick. He's already pawned most of his furnishings except the bed, lounger, and Tel3V. Any money he has left he spends on cigarellas and penny liquor from the quick-shop.

He can't afford the saloons anymore. He is five days late paying his rent. They had shut off his visiphone the week before, and yesterday the power company sent him a FINAL NOTICE memtron.

He figures he'll just bail from his apartment right before they jiglatch his entry lock. He will then live in the shelters, or on the streets, surviving by his wits. Free of all obligations.

Dex pops one of his pornx cards into the media slot on his Tel3V and, wearing nothing but a pair of dirty white boxies, leans back on the lounger. He takes a swig from his last bottle of Krevvar and gazes at the viewer screen.

Soon Dex begins touching himself. How long has it been since he plugged a fem? Too frikkin' long. His passions swelling, he desperately wants release, but his hand refuses to bring him the gratification he so much desires.

His nethers ache. His mind burns.

Dex glances over at the fluffox lying feebly by the front door. Focuses on its bare pink rump.

That's why she named it Pinky.

Oh how he loves Stacia still.

Still aches and burns for her.

And she had once loved him. And Pinky.

Aching and burning.

Pinky never hears him approaching.

Dex straddles the creature from behind, seizes two clumps of its fur, and hoists it from the floor. He then sinks himself into her.

Pinky shrieks like rusty whirling gears.

Dex closes his eyes, plunges deeper.

Stacia... I love you... sooooo much...

Pinky's stalk flails. Its talons claw the air.

I! Love! You!

Dex peaks spectacularly.

He collapses onto his bed sometime after midnight, passing out whilst staring at a crack zigzagging along the ceiling. It reminds him of a lightning bolt, far away and fleeting.

Dex awakens to a flash of pain.

Sharp tiny nails dig into his chest, a warm weight pressing down on him. He groggily opens his eyes to see Pinky's face in front of his own, looking at him.

It is a little known fact—one certainly unknown to Dex—that a small percentage of fluffoxes possess a second vestigial orifice approximately two inches beneath their stalk. When feeling extremely threatened or stressed or angry, they may pry apart the fused flesh to reveal a fully functional gullet and a mouth sporting a broad set of jagged teeth. Meat-eating teeth.

Pinky smiles at Dex.

Then sinks its jaws into his throat.

A week elapses before the building manager, Mister Zevnök, comes to check on his tenant Dex Volga, who reportedly has not been seen for days. And the month's rent is way past due.

Mister Zevnök uses his passpunch to gain entrance. He calls out Dex's name as he creeps into the apartment.

A fluffox greets the lessor, hopping excitedly and tooting its stalk. Zevnök pats its head, notices a brownish crust matting its muzzle. Disgusted, he wipes his hand on his trunks.

"Mr. Volga?" he hails again.

With the fluffox following on his heels, Zevnök surveys the kitchenette, leisure room, lav. Nobody.

Finally, he inspects the bedroom.

He peers into the dimly lit space from the hallway. It takes a moment for his vision to adjust, to recognize what he's seeing. There on the gore-soaked bed is what remains of Dex.

The pet has been well fed.

Out to Pasture

KC Grifant

Daria drove along the I-95 toward Fort Lauderdale in the blinding sunlight, one hand feeling her new heart's steady thump beneath her breastbone.

Her hand dropped and lifted a partially unwrapped burger from the fast food tray on the passenger seat. She appreciated things more since the procedure—food, sunshine, the simple act of driving. She had been given a bill to a long, healthy life.

A cartoon cow smiled up at her from the wrapping as she took a satisfying bite.

She, like many others born with a genetic predisposition to heart failure, had spent a mint on the innovative device.

It was one of many recent breakthroughs in medicine that promised to cut disease and lengthen lives. Media outlets were calling it the dawn of the biomechanical era in history.

And it had all been so easy. One stop at the hospital, an injection of smart nanoparticles, and a few hours of recovery and monitoring. She had watched the particles—white pinpricks on the bedside screen—diffuse throughout her bloodstream before concentrating around her chest. The nanoparticles swiftly arranged themselves into a gleaming casing around her heart that would help pump her blood. A small percentage of additional particles cleaned arteries in the vicinity, "like tiny toothbrushes," the doctor had said. Now, with her mechanically infused heart, she could eat whatever she wanted. She did not need to exercise. She could even smoke once in a while.

"State of the art," she said to herself, and started to hum cheerily as she drove. She was about to take another bite of burger when the sky suddenly darkened.

Tornado, she presumed, her foot braking. Or hurricane. A dense cloud of a uniform beige hovered over the otherwise clear sky. The bun and meat slipped from her fingers.

Up ahead cars were veering off the highway. A metallic crunch screeched behind her. Daria pulled over to the break-down lane, and then over onto the grassy berm. She numbly put the car into park.

The beige had a black dot in the center of it, growing rapidly.

It looked like... like a giant eye. That blinked.

Daria closed her own eyes. She opened them again and it was clearer now: two eyes like muddy lakes, suspended in midair. It was a person's face, rising enormous above the horizon. A miles-wide forehead and a nose like mountain ridges swelling across the blue.

It *must* be a publicity stunt that lets people project faces across the whole skyline, some has-been actor trying to make a comeback. But it wasn't a projection, Daria realized, as a piece of black hair from the face swung and sent a palm tree spinning into the air as if were no sturdier than a toothpick.

The face (some cleverly designed zeppelin?) smeared the sunlight hard before quenching it almost entirely as it grew.

Daria's new heart thudded its rhythmic, reassuring pulse a few beats faster. Figures spilled out of their cars and her seat began to shake. Then the cracks started.

Parts of the ground ripped upward, poles and palm trees shooting into the blackened sky. The highway ahead of Daria tore, and she screamed as a truck slid and launched out of her sight, followed by slabs of asphalt. Chunks of road and sod and trees were falling in reverse, their shadows swirling up toward the hazy, looming face.

"Earthquake!" Daria screamed at the window.

No, not quaking—the earth was fracturing like it was a snow globe rapped against the sharp edge of a table, like one of those round Christmas ornaments slipping and shattering into multiple glass shards.

Daria's hair started to float up, as if she were upside down, and she hysterically tried to smooth it back in place.

The vibrations grew stronger. Her hands thrust for the door, pawing it like an animal until she finally stumbled out.

A diagonal fragment of road and grass fell away from her as the air lifted her up. Her stomach clenched and seemed to plummet through her toes. Through the dust that burned her eyes, she saw a man in gray sweats glide past her, his hook-like prosthetic leg hanging immobile while his flesh leg kicked frantically.

Daria closed her eyes.

I was in a bad car accident, she thought. *Now I'm lying on the side of the road with my new heart bleeding out. I'm unconscious and hallucinating.*

Her lungs felt about ready to burst but still she couldn't breathe. The tickling in her belly reversed and she kicked at the static air until she hit the ground with a soft thud. She opened her eyes, expecting to see the inside of her car, or bloodied pavement. Instead, the lush Florida landscape had turned barren and gloomy, full of this purplish light that stretched out in all directions.

Daria coughed loudly and saw the road had vanished, replaced by a deep, rolling red, like some hellish pasture.

She could discern two cars in the distance, lurid spots against the murk, and a dozen or more people spread far apart. She heard the echo of her cough, the rush of blood through her brain as her heart drummed. It was deafeningly silent around her, until she made out the tinny sound of one of the people screaming. Then nothing.

This isn't Florida, she thought sluggishly as she inhaled the peculiar smell that had no parallel, that made her think of volcanic rock that'd been torn from the bottom of the sea and hurled into space in a fiery clump.

Daria gazed across the field of red and for a minute thought that it was a pool of blood. But when she plunged her hand into the ground it was dry as desiccated bones. A few loosened particles floated upward in the altered gravity.

The profound silence pounded her ear canals and caused her head to swoon. A few people were still picking themselves up, coughing out dust, the sound very distant like they were miles away instead of meters. Somebody, somewhere, was screaming again. Toward the epicenter of the scattering of people were half a dozen of what resembled masks on sticks, jutting out of the red.

Daria recognized the face in the sky as one of the papery masks.

"What the hell?" she said aloud.

A glimmer on the horizon caught her eye. At first she thought it was another version of the giant head, but then the light separated into small, glittery things. She squinted at the disparate shapes, which shifted in fits against the crimson. Bikes, she surmised. Swiveling gears.

Creatures, Daria soon realized. An army of them steadily lumbering toward the humans. They looked like archetypes of robots from old TV shows: round bucket heads, spiny arms, pipes for legs. But they moved—moved like broken spiders, creeping jerkily across the ground.

They tramped nearer, their shadows long and spindly over the dust. Impossible to tell how far off they were, or how large, until they got close to one of the cars.

Twice as tall as Daria, the first of the creatures reached a yellow Mustang, stark against the red landscape. With a sudden burst of agility, it jumped on top of it, an arm-like extension swinging back and forth before shredding through the hood as easily as if it had been constructed of aluminum foil. The other creatures yanked off the tires like taffy candy. Gaping black gaps appeared in front of their chests, and the tires and other auto parts disappeared within them.

Mouths, Daria thought, as remote as the connection was. She pictured a cougar slinking toward grazing deer, hyenas surrounding a dying zebra.

A shudder rocked her body.

The creatures had finished quickly, sweeping back into a broad circle. The Mustang was gone. They resumed their approach, their metallic glint making Daria squint. The other people moved in the opposite direction of the creatures, pressing into the middle of the masks on sticks. She watched a man try to wrench one from the earth. But the stick held firm, the mask frozen in a taunting smile as it flapped.

A gray blur streaked by the periphery of Daria's vision and she turned. It was the man she had seen earlier, his prosthetic leg helping him dash across the red pasture in great strides away from the creatures. A bright spot of silver flashed twice and one of the creatures was next to him, its mouth opening wide.

Daria looked away.

The main group of creatures continued to circle inwards. Two reached another man, a dozen or so yards from her, who also hadn't moved. Sunglasses rested on his brow and headphones dangled around his neck. An armband held his iPod, his hand clutched a cell phone. His face was blank, his lips opening and closing, whispering to himself. Praying.

The creatures encircled the man, withdrawing a moment later, leaving a heap on the ground that looked like a pile of rumpled clothes and two brown loafers. She couldn't tell if any part of him remained in the heap. The headphones, iPod, cell, and sunglasses were gone.

Daria whirled about, scrutinizing all the other people, carrying their phones, cameras, and e-readers. Riding in steel machines, with silicon and plastic attached to their skin and muscles.

And then she knew why the creatures were there.

She dug out her smart phone and earbuds from her jeans and chucked them. They slid along the ground, churning up a slow wave of dust before pitching out into the darkness. The earbuds levitated in the air, like wisps of incense turned tangible.

One of the creatures lunged at her stuff, swallowing it in a shimmer of silver, into its inky chest-maw. But it was too little, too late. They wanted more than just the artificial. They wanted the full combo meal.

The creatures still came.

Run, Daria thought. But there was nowhere to go.

Her heart gave a painful lurch, and the nanoparticles coursing through her bloodstream all seemed to buzz at once.

As the creatures crept toward her, their bodies glistening in whatever alien sunlight shed over this strange world, Daria pressed her hands over her thundering mechanical heart and shut her eyes.

China Doll

Frank Collia

Face down atop the piano, the china doll's painted speck eyes peered over the edge at the keys below, lethal black and ivory rocks taunting it from the bottom of a cliff.

Samantha imagined that if the doll were animate it would jump. Instead, it valued life as only the inanimate can.

Samantha glared at the doll. *I hate all of my things,* she thought, not for the first time today or any other. She hated all of her precious, breakable things. The multi-thousand dollar piano which she couldn't play or even muster enough enthusiasm to try. All her dolls, her toys, her mint condition collectibles that she had no interest in collecting, let alone looking at or even appreciating.

She hated every thing that surrounded her: this room, the house. Her family. She hated how her mother called her Sam despite being the one who named her Samantha, as if the time needed to speak the other two syllables could be banked for use later in life. Life after Samantha.

Because this couldn't go on forever.

Her parents' voices echoed down the hallway from the kitchen.

"She's a good girl." Her father.

"We're so far past that now, aren't we?" Her mother.

Samantha pinged the piano's C8 key with her pinky, the highest-pitch note punctuating the silent beats between her parents' volley of excuses and accusations.

"I don't understand it," said her father.

Ping.

"Of course you don't," said her mother. "You won't."

Ping.

"But…"

"But what?"

"But she's our daughter."

"What does that change?"

Ping. Ping ping ping ping ping.

Samantha slid off the vinyl-upholstered piano bench, walked halfway across the living room, and stopped. Today she was wearing a frilly blue dress and shiny black shoes. She looked down at the chain around her ankle, then at the other end attached to the iron eyebolt embedded in the far wall.

What does that change? she thought. Nothing.

The shouting from the kitchen ceased and now she was listening to the footsteps slowly approaching, until they got within a few feet of her door. As close as they ever got. Close enough.

"Samantha? Honey? Are you hungry?"

Her father never called her Sam. She thought if she could love she would love him for that reason alone.

"No."

"*You* haven't eaten in a while."

She didn't answer.

She didn't know how far he planned to play out this little domestic delusion, but she did not see the need to enable him further. She had already said more than necessary.

"Okay, hon," he said, his voice a cracked whisper.

Samantha listened to him return to the kitchen. She knew what came next.

"What?" he said.

"Nothing," said her mother.

"Oh, don't give me that. What do you want me to do?"

"Your job?"

Samantha tuned out the rest. The words differed, but the theme of their "discussions" re-ran itself tediously. She lied down on the plush, patterned rug and waited for their daily routine to march its following step.

"What would you even say if she told you that she was hungry?" Her mother.

"Let's just get this over with."

"No, really, tell me. What would you say?"

"She wouldn't say that."

"Then why do you ask?"

Samantha shut her eyes. Her father had told her the gas they pumped into the room at this time each day contained medicine for her. She'd never smelled a thing nor had any recollection of being knocked out. She didn't care. She only wished she could enjoy the unconsciousness.

Her mother had been blunter. She said they designed the gas to alter her genetic code, each day's dose tweaked a bit based on the previous day's readings. So far, they hadn't had much success. Samantha knew they hadn't had any. She also knew they never would.

"Sam, are you awake?"

It had happened again. Samantha opened her eyes and stretched her arms. She could see the cameras so she knew they could see her. Why, then, did her mother insist on always asking that question? Was it on her checklist? Did one of her battery of tests somehow reveal Samantha detested the shortened version of her name, and her mother intentionally used it as passive-aggressive vengeance for her being stuck in this pointless cycle?

A smile curled up the corners of Samantha's mouth. She asked herself these same redundant questions every time, too. *Like mother, like daughter,* she thought.

"Very well, Sam," said her mother. She always said that, too. Only the next part changed. "Your visitor today is named Toni Mattocks."

Samantha sat up on the floor and turned to the chair by the window. The woman seated there tilted her head toward the speaker in the ceiling.

"It's Antoinette, actually," she said, grinning at the disembodied voice.

Samantha laughed aloud. *My mother.*

"And you must be—"

"Samantha."

"You can call me Ms. Mattocks."

This one looked older than the last one. Same color hair, though longer and wavier. Slightly fatter, but still within the strictly-controlled average. She had dark skin, the darkest yet. Samantha considered what difference that would make.

As usual, as if ingrained in the process itself, Samantha wondered what her parents looked like. Had they made any efforts to resemble her, or more accurately, vice versa? Would that have made their jobs easier? Harder? She didn't think it made any difference to her father.

"Do you know why I'm here, Samantha?"

Samantha nodded. The same reason they all came. Her father explained it was the only way they could tell if the latest dosage had worked.

If it fixed her.

"How are you feeling today, Samantha?"

Samantha stood and faced Ms. Mattocks, her back to the closed door, the only way out of the room. She felt fine, but then she wasn't the problem.

"They tell me you're eight."

"Eight what?"

Ms. Mattocks produced a hesitant chuckle. "I remember when my own little girl was that age."

Starting to feel lightheaded, Samantha spread her feet for better balance.

"I taught her and I'm hoping to teach you, too."

"What can you teach me?"

"I've been tutoring math for near thirty years now."

"Math?"

"That's right."

"The last one was a piano teacher." Samantha yawned, then flexed her jaw.

Ms. Mattocks' laughter flowed smoother. "And I've faced thirty years of yawns, too. At first. But I have a secret. Want to hear it?"

"I have a secret, too," said Samantha.

"*Sam.*" Her mother's voice.

"That's okay," said Ms. Mattocks. "Girls should have secrets. Am I right, Sam?"

"Samantha."

"Sorry. *Samantha*. How about we make a deal? I'll tell you my secret and, if you'd like, you can tell me yours?"

"What's your secret?" asked Samantha.

Ms. Mattocks placed a cupped hand beside her mouth. "Math can be a lot of fun."

Samantha pursed her lips.

"What's wrong, sweetie?" asked Ms. Mattocks.

"Now it's not a secret."

"Why?"

"Because someone else knows. Nobody else is supposed to know your secret."

Samantha yawned again.

"Are you tired?"

"Maybe."

"Were you sleeping on the floor when I came in?" asked Ms. Mattocks, shifting her weight between the chair's arms.

"Was I sleeping?"

"You were on the floor with your eyes closed."

"But was I sleeping?"

Ms. Mattocks lowered her gaze to Samantha's foot while keeping her forced grin in place.

"Does that chain hurt?"

"Please stick to the script, Sam." Her mother.

Ms. Mattocks leaned forward and in a hushed voice said, "I can ask them about the chain, Samantha."

Samantha's mother's voice barked through the speaker. "Ms. Mattocks."

The tutor extended her open palms. "I can help you if you let me."

"I can't let you," said Samantha.

"Why not?"

"Because I won't be here."

"Ms. Mattocks, would you be so kind as to open the window behind you?" asked Samantha's mother, her tone very nearly pleasant.

Ms. Mattocks glanced up at the speaker, then back to the window. She smiled at Samantha. "How long has it been since you've had some fresh air in here?"

Samantha's right eye twitched.

Shunting the chair out of the way, Ms. Mattocks looked over her shoulder at Samantha. "We'll get you some sunlight in here, too. Nothing like sunshine for you."

The woman pulled the curtains aside and raised the blinds. A framed pane of glass hung between her and the wall. She paused as her comprehension caught up with her vision. The blinds dropped. She stepped away.

"Toni," sighed Samantha's mother. "Did you even read your waiver?"

"Why isn't there a window?"

"There *is* a window," said Samantha's mother. "Just not a real window."

"Why would you hang a sheet of glass on the wall?"

"No one ever opens the window like they say," said Samantha.

"And why would you bother hanging curtains?" asked Ms. Mattocks.

"Distraction," said Samantha's mother.

"Where am I?" asked Ms. Mattocks, her voice struggling.

"Oh, you know very well where you are, Toni," said Samantha's mother. "Now sit down."

"I want to leave now."

"Doesn't anyone read the waiver?!"

"What waiver?" Hands trembling, Ms. Mattocks reached through the blinds and tapped on the glass. "All I signed was a work agreement."

"Right. That. That's what we have to call it." Her father. "No one would sign *a waiver*. A bit suspicious."

"That's enough out of you," said Samantha's mother.

Ms. Mattocks dashed for the door and tried the knob. Locked. She shook her fist at the speaker. "Now! Let me out now!" She circled around in front of Samantha and crouched eye level with her. "Please?"

But Samantha had gone. The creature, anchored some-where inside Samantha, unfurled from her mouth, splashing its bulk onto the rug in a puddle of saliva, mucus, and blood. Her mother had described it as a cross between a worm and an eel (but with legs, her father added). She admitted to it being a loose analogy, her zoological points of reference sadly limited to Earth.

Ms. Mattocks fell into the chair, thrust herself back as far as she could go.

She covered her face and screamed through her fingers.

The creature reared up, spraying forth a thick mist. Ms. Mattocks registered the cool shower on her skin and felt her body grow heavy. She tried to lower her hands, but couldn't. She tried to move, but every limb, every muscle felt clenched, rigid.

"What…" Her parted lips froze. "Are… you?" The words escaping on her final breath.

The creature expanded, splitting itself down the underside of its long, narrow trunk, into a gaping mouth the length of its body. It enveloped its victim, mincing Ms. Mattocks, clothes and bones included, with row upon row of tiny razor teeth, leaving nothing remaining on the chair except a film of viscous spittle.

And even that would be gone by the time Samantha had returned.

She did not remember her transformation, or how she ended up back at the piano. She always seemed to end up back at the piano. Always, of course, being a relative term. She existed outside of a linear perception of time. Later, before, now—they all circled back to here.

Samantha slammed her fingers down on the keys. The china doll, still precariously perched, jumped, exposing its nose to the air below. Samantha pounded the keys again. The doll jolted closer to the edge.

Again. Closer.

Again. Closer.

And again.

The doll teetered for a moment then tumbled, clearing the keys, striking Samantha's thigh, and falling to the rug, its porcelain face facing up.

Samantha had no true understanding of the creature, but her father reassured her that was not unusual with a parasite. *Her* parasite.

Or maybe it was the other way around.

She pushed back the bench and stared down at the doll. It stared back. She lifted her foot and brought down her heel right in the middle of its blank, glazed face. Shattering it.

I hate all of my things, she thought, not for the first time today or any other.

Nighty Night

Lisamarie Lamb

"Sleep," said Ajay, with a smug and satisfied expression, "is for the weak and unimportant. I am neither of these things." And with that he sank down into the sofa, crossed his legs, and placed his hands behind his head. "Therefore, I no longer intend to sleep."

His friend—more like acquaintance, sometime colleague, and the only person slow enough not to think of an excuse when Ajay suggested drinks at the snobby new wine bar that evening—Carla pressed her lips together and nodded.

She hadn't really been listening, didn't really care, and wasn't in the mood to make small talk.

All Carla wanted was a glass of wine (a cheaper, colder, tastier one than the stuff sitting in front of her, supposedly aged just right and stored for years and totally wasted on her), and a long hot bath, and possibly something to eat. Maybe. That was for later.

For now, she was stuck in this awful bar and she had to sit next to The Creep.

The Creep. That's what they called Ajay behind his back. In front of his face, too, if the need arose. Always sucking up to the boss, always trying to be one step ahead of everyone else. Always thinking himself better than everyone.

The Creep was a fitting sobriquet.

He was called worse things too. Choice words that Carla didn't like to think about most of the time. But when it came to Ajay, she made an exception, and the words were rolling around in her head right now, tumbling over one another in their eagerness to make themselves the nom du jour.

Ajay raised his eyebrows and looked Carla straight in the face, stared deep into her eyes, and she felt sure he knew exactly what she was thinking. Her cheeks reddened and she took a gulp of her wine to hide her blushes behind something.

But Ajay knew nothing of Carla's thoughts. Of course he didn't. If anything, he would have assumed the woman he was having drinks with was impressed with his confidence, his poise. His cool manliness. They all were. He was a prince among frogs.

Especially with his new position and his new—what to call it? Superpower, perhaps? Or was it more of an ability? The problem was, the first description made it sound too magical, too unreal, and the second was just stupid. It was no more an ability than flying was, or becoming invisible. Not everyone could do it, no one could really do it, even if everyone wished they could.

No. *Ability* wasn't the right word for it.

Not that it mattered right this second. Nor was it his to call anything yet anyway. He had tests to perform and checks to pass. But that was for the coming weeks, and would detract from his extraordinary tale. A tale he hoped would persuade this woman with him (was it Carly? Kathy? Something like that) into bed with him. Not that she looked like that much fun, but sometimes it was the quiet ones after all.

And she was knocking back the wine.

"So then," said Ajay, stretching out a bit, moving closer to Carla. "Do you want to know what I am going to do?" He glanced at her almost empty glass. "And would you care for another?"

Carla was jolted out of her nice bubble bath daydream by Ajay's voice, but not his words. She tried and failed to work out what he had just said to her. But since he was nodding towards her drink, she had to assume. She shook her head.

"I'm driving back. I shouldn't really have had this one. It was a bigger glass than I thought."

"Really?" Ajay was also driving, but that wasn't going to stop him. He had ordered the expensive bottle of thirty-year-old vino, so he wasn't about to waste it or suffer the ignominy of asking for the cork so he could take it home. Not what was done here, so his boss had told him when he brought him here for that meeting.

That very important meeting. That incredible day.

"Really," Carla assured him, her eyes shifting to the clock above the bar and then to the door. She fretted over her car, parked outside, a little too far from the curb but close enough not to warrant another go at getting it right. "Anyway, I don't tend to drink that much," she lied.

"That's a shame," murmured Ajay in what he hoped was a seductive tone. "I bought this especially for you."

He indicated that damned bottle again, and Carla rolled her eyes, irritated now.

"Well you should have asked. It tastes like crap." But she drank the rest of her glass nonetheless, and wondered if she could sneak one more swallow if Ajay ever got up off his skinny arse and went to have a piss or something. Yes, it did taste like crap, but it had a nice buzz about it.

Ajay's face—his mouth an 'O' of surprise, his eyes just as round, his forehead wrinkled and suddenly older than it should have been—told her she might have gone too far, even if it was the truth, and Carla, a kind soul in a hard shell, regretted everything up to that point. She imagined she'd probably regret things beyond this point too, but if she could limit the damage at least she could look at Ajay on Monday morning with a small smile of mutual remorse instead of not meeting the man's eyes at all.

"Sorry, Ajay, I'm sorry. I shouldn't have said that. It was cruel. It was unnecessary. Really, can we start again?" Carla did not want to start again, but she was grateful to see that Ajay's shock lessened as she spoke.

The man nodded. "Of course." But his tone was cold and his spine was stiff and the wind had been punched out of him.

Carla cleared her throat. "What was it you wanted to tell me? It sounded intriguing." It hadn't, of course, because he'd barely said a word about whatever it was, but now she was mollifying the man beside her.

Ajay uncrossed his legs and sat slightly more upright. He looked at the other patrons in the crowded room, then at the woman he was sharing the evening with. A memory flashed across his mind, reached out with its spindly fingers, and shut his mouth.

"Oh, nothing. Much. Nothing much. I mean, I was just saying that I thought sleep was overrated. That's all. Nothing interesting."

Carla nodded. He was right. It was nothing interesting. She picked up her handbag from the floor and riffled through it, searching for her keys.

"Okay." How much would a taxi be? It was Friday, after all. "I'll have another glass."

Ajay smiled. He poured. Maybe he'd tell her about his new capability after all.

After Ajay and Carla had drunk the rest of that bottle and most of another one (although not of the same vintage, still supposedly a superb year), after they had staggered to Ajay's car and wobbled into his apartment, after they had fallen into bed and rutted uselessly for a while, Ajay could no longer keep his secret to himself. Partly to assuage the embarrassment of his failure in bed, and partly because he had to tell someone, anyone, the first one he could, and there really was no one else to share it with.

He lay in the dark and then nudged Carla's arm. She mumbled something, incoherent strings of consonants that melded together into an acknowledgement.

"Do you want to know my secret?"

Carla may have nodded. Ajay thought she did. She'd twitched a little, so he continued telling his story.

"The boss asked me to help him. And he offered me a promotion. So I wanted to celebrate. Nobody wanted to come except you, but that's okay. They'll see. They'll see when the operation is done and I'm so powerful and so much better than them. They'll see then."

Ajay poked Carla's arm. She blinked in the filmy semi-darkness, the air thick with body odour and musty sheets. "Are you listening? It doesn't matter. The boss offered me a chance at something, something great, something incredible. He will send me to a doctor, and the doctor will do something to me, do something to my head, my brain, and I won't have to sleep anymore. So I'll be able to work. More. I'll be able to work more and do more and be more. I'll take over the company some day, that's what the boss said. That's what he wants."

There was a loud snort beside him, then a grunt and a groan. Carla was asleep, hadn't heard a word he said, was already dreaming about being somewhere else with someone else. And Ajay, knowing it would be one of the last times, let sleep take him too. He wondered whether he would miss it.

Carla awoke first, peeling her eyes open and grimacing in the far too bright morning light. She could still taste the previous night's wine on her gums and tongue and wanted more. Even the dizzying sickness that was creeping over her wasn't enough to put her off.

Ajay snored massively, inhaling the dust motes that hung around the room. Carla, suddenly acutely aware of everything—every drunken fumble, every lewd whisper—slipped from the bed, from the bedroom, gathering up her clothes and shoes and her bag when she found it, and then she was out of the door, the chill slapping her in the face and making everything much better and much, much worse than it had been.

Monday morning came brutally quick. It brought with it different things for different people—good, bad, and ugly— but nothing quite as different as what it brought for Ajay. He arrived at work early, too excited to sleep, unconcerned with the weariness that now weighed heavy upon his shoulders.

He wouldn't have to think about it soon.

Carla arrived early as well. But then, she always did. Ajay may have been The Creep, but Carla was The Swot. Quiet, keeping to herself. She just got on with it, plodding onwards, hoping to reach a point where someone somewhere noticed her. Hopefully the right person. Never a chance of burnout for her, but even so, she felt aggrieved that bloody Ajay was being offered something so impossible. So extraordinary.

She had heard what he had said.

She may have been hammered, as good as unconscious, but his words slid into her brain nonetheless, and when she awoke they had remained intact. Unfathomable, ridiculous, yet somehow believable.

Carla wanted that chance too. It was about time. And if she wasn't going to be offered it, she would have to ask for it. She had been unable to think of anything else all weekend, and now could put her plan into action. She wasn't sure she could. Especially when she saw Ajay, his face drawn, his eyes circled with the shadowy bruises of exhaustion. She would be stealing this from him, his dream, his future. Possibly. Surely she would be. This had to be a one-off, didn't it?

Carla almost changed her mind.

She almost slinked back to her desk, almost hid behind her stacks of paperwork, almost had her head down, carrying on and forgetting about it all.

Almost.

She would have if Ajay hadn't spotted her and waved at her and winked. He strutted over and punched his hands into his pockets, stood there in front of her rocking in his shiny brown shoes. All semblance of the man Carla thought he might have been—if only for a drunken instant—was now gone, and The Creep, all nonsense and bluster and cockiness, had been restored.

"You all right, Carrie?"

Carla flushed without her wanting to, knowing Ajay was taunting her because surely he *had* known her name. "Carla," she said with as little emotion as she could manage. It was still too much. Her voice was higher than she intended it to be and her name broke as it crossed her lips.

"Carla. Of course." He smiled, big teeth beaming in her face. "So, Friday…"

Carla knew what was coming. She braced herself for the withering remark.

"Yes?"

"Friday… we were both pretty drunk, yes? Both really out of it. So maybe it's best if we just forget about it? All of it?"

He tried another smile, and Carla could see the nerves beneath. She realised it wasn't just the limp sex he was talking about.

"There's not much to forget," she said, giving his crotch an icy stare. "So, whatever."

"Fine then. It's just I—"

Carla cut him off with a hand flicked in the air. "Is this going to take long? I've got things to do."

Ajay closed his mouth and shook his head, chastened. Before he could say or do anything else, Carla had confidently stalked off. She *would* take his future. She *would* take his company. She *would* take his sleeplessness.

Carla, nervous now, terrified actually, and trembling, her breath pumping hard against her ribs, tightening her chest, kept walking. She approached the boss's door, an enormous, completely out-of-place, and utterly exaggerated piece of hewn ebony that had no purpose other than to prove, with no room for doubts, that Mr. O'Dell *was* the boss. Who else would work behind such an impressive door? Rather, doors. A double monstrosity, although Carla had only ever seen the right half open.

She knocked, her knuckles aching against the rigidity of the wood. She blew on them. She knocked again, even more scared to now because it might enrage Mr. O'Dell, but she couldn't wait any longer. This time she was rewarded with a gruff, irritated voice from the other side of the door.

"What is it?"

"Mr. O'Dell, my name's Carla Winchester. I need to speak with you."

"No." The boss went completely silent.

Carla raised her hand to knock again and as she did so she saw the lanky form of Ajay padding down the corridor. He saw her, their eyes met, and there was more than a shifty embarrassment there now. Ajay knew. He knew what she wanted, what she was doing. He paled, his loping strides breaking into a run, his arms outstretched to stop Carla from entering that room, from saying anything at all to O'Dell.

"Sir, it's about Ajay Kapresh. His recent opportunity."

Ajay was closing now. The corridor wasn't an especially long one, far too short now for Carla's liking. She tried again, just as Ajay's hand clamped around her wrist and yanked her backwards.

"About his operation!" she shouted desperately, her wrist bones cracking under the steel grip that Ajay had managed to latch onto her with.

"Jesus, Ajay, let go of me, you absolute shit!"

"What are you doing, Carla?" Ajay hissed. "Just what the fuck do you think you're up to?" He twisted her hand back on itself, the tendons straining beneath her skin. She tried to pull her arm away, but Ajay was too strong in his anger. "Don't. Just don't. Not to me. I deserve this." He paused, his grasp never loosening. "Is this because of Friday night? Is that it? I can make it up to you, if that's what you want."

Carla shook her head, the sharp pain clearing her mind. If ever she had doubted what she'd planned to do, she could abandon that doubt now.

But before she could answer, before she could really tell Ajay what she wanted to, the massive doors opened and Mr. O'Dell stepped out. His light grey eyes appraised the situation transpiring in his hallway.

"Let go."

Two words full of menace, and Ajay did as he was told.

"In." To Carla. "Go." To Ajay.

Two more words and their meaning was huge, a heaping serving of disappointment and disgust aimed at both of the shamefaced employees quarrelling in the hallway.

With a final look of despair, Ajay hung his head, scuffed his shiny shoes along the carpet, and departed.

Carla did not watch him go. She couldn't. She hadn't wanted this to happen. Not exactly this anyway. Even if Ajay was a complete bastard who deserved everything he got.

"So, he told you about his promotion then." Definitely no question in that voice, and definitely no pleasure. Mr. O'Dell gestured roughly in the direction of a straight-backed, wooden chair with no cushion. Carla assumed she should sit on it, and did so, crossing her legs primly, forgetting she was supposed to be saying something.

"Well?" O'Dell wouldn't let her forget so easily.

"Oh, yes. He—Ajay—mentioned something about something." Not good enough. O'Dell's eyebrows creased and a frown took over his already glowering face. "I meant to say, he said something about not sleeping. Not needing to sleep. That you could do that for him."

Had she said too much?

Carla's palms sweated, and her stomach churned her breakfast to the extent that she thought it might erupt all over Mr. O'Dell's regal desk.

A profoundly disturbing thought lodged itself in Carla's mind. Ajay was lying. He had to be. He had made the whole thing up to get her into bed, to sound interesting enough for her to sleep with him (and look how that had panned out), and the reason he had been so afraid of her speaking with the boss was that he would be found out to be a total bullshitter.

Carla's cheeks reddened. She couldn't get comfortable, her legs dangling there. So she uncrossed them, then crossed them the other way, had this horrible notion she was trying something Sharon Stone-esque when that was the very last thing she wanted to do, and gave up.

"Mr. O'Dell, sir, I'm sorry to have wasted your time. I'm sorry for the… situation in the hallway, and I'm sorry that I said anything at all about anything so ludicrous. I just would really like to go now and forget it. All of it. Every piece."

Carla's rambling speech had sucked the wind out of her and although she tried to rise, she couldn't. She was stuck half in, half out of the least comfortable chair in the world and her boss was scowling at her, his chubby face registering repugnance.

"It's Carla, isn't it?"

The question surprised Carla, and she sank back down into the seat, nodding.

O'Dell nodded too, and he opened a drawer in his desk, pulling out a load of papers.

"If you do want to go ahead with this, I need you to sign here." He pointed to a line of dots with his pen. "And if you do not, I'll need you to sign this contract instead." Another gesture, another line. "If it's the latter, you mustn't disclose anything about the experiment to anyone. Right? You have to keep quiet and act as though nothing unusual is going on. Unlike Ajay. You telling me he told you tells me he has breached our contract. His and mine."

Carla blinked at the second set of dots. She was tempted by them, could see herself taking the boss's pen, scribbling her name across and running away, hiding in her cubicle in the hopes that no one would ever notice her again.

But she didn't move.

When he was sure he had her hooked, O'Dell continued. "But if you sign the former contract, agree to the operation, agree to never sleeping again, agree to using that time which would have been squandered being unconscious to instead work for me, to be more productive, then we have a deal. You still tell no one though."

Carla's mouth ran dry.

It was true. Everything Ajay had told her was true!

"Ajay signed the first one. He would have been having his operation right about..." O'Dell checked his gold Rolex. "Now."

"I'll sign it." Her voice was not her own. It was croaky and full of something unfamiliar to her.

"Which one?"

The second one, forget it, it's preposterous, not worth it.

"The first one. I'll do it. I'll have the operation."

A smile spread across O'Dell's face, the first Carla had ever seen there.

"Right. Sign it." He passed her the pen.

"I haven't read it."

O'Dell shrugged. "I have told you what's in it, there's not much else. That's the important part anyway. You can read the rest afterwards."

No, no, no. Nonono.

Carla accepted the pen and wrote out her name with a quaking hand.

And it was done.

"Come on then, let's get going. The doctor's expecting us."

Carla gasped. "What? Now? Right now?"

O'Dell didn't answer but clutched her elbow and led her from his office, up the corridor, into the lift. Down, down, down further than she had ever been before. Down into the sub-basement, said to be only for junk storage, a tomb of obsolete printers and dead photocopiers.

And Ajay, shredded and shattered, watched Carla and O'Dell as they went, as Carla took his place, going down to the makeshift operating theatre that had been reserved for him.

When Carla opened her eyes, she was at home. And everything was the same. She felt rested and a bit hungover in a gentle, enveloping way. There was a note on her bedside table, and a cheque. A big cheque. The note was a thank you from O'Dell, for being the first "volunteer" in his new project, a project which, if successful, would revolutionise the way work was done. No more nine-to-five, no more overtime. It would be constant, a complete way of life.

Carla had to admit to having slight anxiety about the "if successful" part, but she kept it to herself. And when the boss visited her in her own home, when he brought her flowers and a doctor to check her over, she felt special and loved and successful. They didn't stay long, of course. The doctor was paid by the half hour, and O'Dell had people to see and places to be, which meant that Carla had no time to ask any of the questions that were ricocheting around her brain. Questions such as, why did she still feel tired? She had thought that removing the need to sleep would automatically remove the feeling of drowsiness that accompanied it. It seemed she was wrong.

But it was good of them to come, nonetheless.

When she felt a little more like herself, when the tiny scar across her forehead was less red and less swollen, she phoned her parents and told them about her promotion, neglecting to mention the part about having her brain fiddled with. No, they didn't need to hear that. Getting on in her job was enough for them, and they were pleased and proud and Carla felt better than ever.

Aside from the headache.

It was dull and incessant, seeping down from the top of her skull, creeping along her neck, and slipping down her spine. Pills didn't cure it. Alcohol numbed it briefly, but once her veins were purely blood again, there it was, knock knock knocking, refusing to be ignored.

But Carla had to ignore it. She had work to do. Lots of work. Mountains of it.

Which was good.

It *was* good. It really was.

She felt well and healthy and was *getting stuff done*. Even if tiredness was a problem.

Six weeks after the operation, four weeks after returning to work full time (and, according to her new contract, full time now meant twenty-four hours a day, five days a week— weekends were her own, the company was fair like that), Carla's colleagues noticed a few things about her.

Firstly, she looked terrible. Bloodshot-eyed and grey-skinned, she shuffled from desk to desk, gathering this and that, looking unsure as to what it was she was supposed to be doing but doing it anyway, smiling a taut, almost frightened smile at anyone who tried to speak with her or engage with her in any way.

Secondly, she never seemed to leave. She was the first one there in the morning, last one there at night. Her chair seemed to have moulded itself around her, and there were deep grooves in the thin carpet beneath it, where feet were swung back and forth, back and forth, for hours upon hours.

It was strange.

And she wouldn't talk about it.

People she had once considered her friends began to stay away, afraid of her now, this odd, new Carla with the crazed eyes and fixed frown.

Carla didn't care. Mr. O'Dell would sometimes pass by her desk and catch her eye. Occasionally he smiled at her, and it was then that she remembered why she was doing this. Prestige, rewards, recognition. Surely this was what it was all about. Surely.

But the headache... it thumped now, pulsing in a vicious rhythm that never ended and screamed through her body, a tornado of pain. She desperately wanted to close her eyes and let sleep take her. She missed it more than she thought she would. She hadn't realised how much she enjoyed just lying down and letting herself go. It had seemed so pointless then. Now, the memory of it was beautiful beyond measure.

When she shut her stinging eyelids, she was blessed with a moment of relief, an instant in which the angry throbbing ceased and she was lifted away from everything. And then it returned with a vengeance, smacking her across the face to remind her that it was there. As if she could forget.

Other than O'Dell, Ajay was the only one who knew what was really happening, and he did not dare mention it. He had a job to protect, after all. He did needle Carla in passing though, asking her if she was sleeping well, or if he could help out with her ever increasing pile of work. All Carla could do was glare at him, hatred trying to beam out of her glazed eyes, so sunken now that a quick glance in the right light gave the observer the idea that there were no eyes there at all, just deep, dark holes.

After another month—Carla was now barely moving, awake but hardly functioning, her body trying to give up on her, her brain not letting it, a battle that raged beneath her bones and tearing her apart—Ajay bounced into the chair next to Carla's and nudged her. She turned slowly, carefully, her head so heavy that she thought—hoped—that it might topple from her shoulders and relieve the agony.

"What?" she rasped, hooking her irritability behind the word. She could manage one syllable. Asking any more of her was asking too much.

Ajay grinned and pointed to his forehead, his hairline, where a faint red mark, neater and smoother than her own scar, lay across it. It was tiny. No one would notice it. Carla's eyebrows raised and she tilted her head to one side, adept now at questioning without words because words hurt.

"Oh, yes," confirmed Ajay. "I got it done. But the thing is, I took the initiative, Carla. I went private. Took everything I had. Every penny, my house, my car, everything, but it's done. And guess what?"

"What?" Carla groaned.

"I'm not tired."

"What?" Same word, different meaning.

Ajay burst out a snorting laugh and leaned back in his stolen seat. "Look at my eyes. See any red? Any lines? Any bags? No, you don't. And you won't. Technology and science have moved forward since you, darling, and money does a lot of talking."

He was right. His eyes were bright, the whites lustrous. His skin glowed. He looked good.

And Carla, beneath her leaden eyelids, could not bear it. She tried to stand, tried to launch herself at the mocking man beside her, but she did not have the energy for it. She could not wrap her feeble fingers around his neck and squeeze the life out of him even though that was the only image her mind would permit at that moment.

Bastard.

She tried to think of other descriptors, but her brain was failing her.

So… *bastard, bastard, bastard.*

Carla felt tears dribbling down her cheeks. She hadn't realised she was crying. "O'Dell," she gurgled, her lips numb as the name spilled across them.

Ajay winked at her. "I'll take you myself."

With the stares of the rest of the staff on the two of them, Ajay hoisted Carla from her chair and propelled her out of the room, down the corridor, quickly, too fast for her feet. They were dragging behind, her toes crushed within her once pretty high heels. She didn't so much as whimper. And when Ajay rapped on the boss's door then stepped aside, leaving Carla slumped against it as though drunk, she said nothing, didn't even try.

The door opened and Carla keeled over into the office, landed with a thud on O'Dell's plush carpet, and stayed there, sobbing.

"Tired."

She said that one word, heard it muffled by the carpet, and cried harder. They hadn't said anything. Hadn't said that this would happen, that she would want to die rather than live 24/7.

"Shut the door, Ajay," ordered O'Dell. "And wait outside."

Ajay, as ever, did as he was told.

Now it was just Carla and the boss, the latter hovering over the former, watching the broken body with the broken brain as it curled in on itself, craving the one thing it couldn't have.

"I can't undo it, you know. It can't be reversed." O'Dell paused, letting this information sink in. "It was all in the contract."

Carla concentrated on breathing and smelling the carpet. It smelled good, clean and fresh.

"A contract which," continued O'Dell, "I'm sure you'd read thoroughly."

Carla couldn't remember. Had she? Did it matter now? She nodded slightly anyway, certain that was what O'Dell wanted.

"Right, well, since you read the contract, you know what happens should you fall below expectations. If your output decreases and so forth."

Her addled mind did attempt to recall. It didn't recover anything.

O'Dell knelt down, his old knees popping one after the other. He scooped Carla up and threw her into the chair she had signed the contract in.

"You're no good to me anymore, and I can't risk you going to a hospital or they'll know what we're doing here. The competition might find out and that cannot be allowed to happen. Besides, I've got Ajay now. He's got initiative, I'll give him that."

O'Dell opened his desk drawer and brought out a syringe filled with orange liquid. He delicately pressed the plunger until a single short squirt of the stuff shot out.

"Don't worry, Carla. I'm going to put you to sleep."

Carla smiled. A genuine, happy smile.

"Thank you," she said.

When it was all over, when her ragged breathing had stopped and O'Dell could detect no pulse, he poked his head out of his office door and nodded at Ajay.

"I've got a job for you."

Ajay sighed with pleasure. He was back where he was supposed to be, at the top, O'Dell's right hand man. Always. Twenty-four hours a day.

As Ajay dragged Carla's body from O'Dell's office, up the corridor, to the service lift where he would take it to the basement and burn it in the furnace, he smiled. He blinked. He rubbed his eyes lightly. They stung a little. He shook it off. It was nothing.

The lift doors closed.

The ride down was peaceful. Calm.

Ajay yawned.

The Horror
of the Heights
Sir Arthur Conan Doyle

The idea that the extraordinary narrative which has been called the Joyce-Armstrong Fragment is an elaborate practical joke evolved by some unknown person, cursed by a perverted and sinister sense of humour, has now been abandoned by all who have examined the matter. The most macabre and imaginative of plotters would hesitate before linking his morbid fancies with the unquestioned and tragic facts which reinforce the statement. Though the assertions contained in it are amazing and even monstrous, it is none the less forcing itself upon the general intelligence that they are true, and that we must readjust our ideas to the new situation. This world of ours appears to be separated by a slight and precarious margin of safety from a most singular and unexpected danger. I will endeavour in this narrative, which reproduces the original document in its necessarily somewhat fragmentary form, to lay before the reader the whole of the facts up to date, prefacing my statement by saying that, if there be any who doubt the narrative of Joyce-Armstrong, there can be no question at all as to the facts concerning Lieutenant Myrtle, R. N., and Mr. Hay Connor, who undoubtedly met their end in the manner described.

The Joyce-Armstrong Fragment was found in the field which is called Lower Haycock, lying one mile to the westward of the village of Withyham, upon the Kent and Sussex border. It was on the 15th of September last that an agricultural labourer, James Flynn, in the employment of Mathew Dodd, farmer, of the Chauntry Farm, Withyham, perceived a briar pipe lying near the footpath which skirts the hedge in Lower Haycock. A few paces farther on he picked up a pair of broken binocular glasses. Finally, among some nettles in the ditch, he caught sight of a flat, canvas-backed book, which proved to be a note-book with detachable leaves, some of which had come loose and were fluttering along the base of the hedge. These he collected, but some, including the first, were never recovered, and leave a deplorable hiatus in this all-important statement. The note-book was taken by the labourer to his master, who in turn showed it to Dr. J. H. Atherton, of Hartfield. This gentleman at once recognized the need for an expert exam-ination, and the manuscript was forwarded to the Aero Club in London, where it now lies.

The first two pages of the manuscript are missing. There is also one torn away at the end of the narrative, though none of these affect the general coherence of the story. It is conjectured that the missing opening is concerned with the record of Mr. Joyce-Armstrong's qualifications as an aeronaut, which can be gathered from other sources and are admitted to be unsurpassed among the air-pilots of England. For many years he has been looked upon as among the most daring and the most intellectual of flying men, a combination which has enabled him to both invent and test several new devices, including the common gyroscopic attachment which is known by his name. The main body of the manuscript is written neatly in ink, but the last few lines are in pencil and are so ragged as to be hardly legible—exactly, in fact, as they might be expected to appear if they were scribbled off hurriedly from the seat of a moving aeroplane. There are, it may be added, several stains, both on the last page and on the outside cover, which have been pronounced by the Home Office experts to be blood—probably human and certainly mammalian. The fact that something closely resembling the organism of malaria was discovered in this blood, and that Joyce-Armstrong is known to have suffered from intermittent fever, is a remarkable example of the new weapons which modern science has placed in the hands of our detectives.

And now a word as to the personality of the author of this epoch-making statement. Joyce-Armstrong, according to the few friends who really knew something of the man, was a poet and a dreamer, as well as a mechanic and an inventor. He was a man of considerable wealth, much of which he had spent in the pursuit of his aeronautical hobby. He had four private aeroplanes in his hangars near Devizes, and is said to have made no fewer than one hundred and seventy ascents in the course of last year. He was a retiring man with dark moods, in which he would avoid the society of his fellows. Captain Dangerfield, who knew him better than anyone, says that there *were times when his eccentricity threatened to develop into something more serious. His habit of carrying a shot-gun with him in his aeroplane was one manifestation of it.*

Another was the morbid effect which the fall of Lieutenant Myrtle had upon his mind. Myrtle, who was attempting the height record, fell from an altitude of something over thirty thousand feet. Horrible to narrate, his head was entirely obliterated, though his body and limbs preserved their configuration. At every gathering of airmen, Joyce-Armstrong, according to Dangerfield, would ask, with an enigmatic smile: "And where, pray, is Myrtle's head?"

On another occasion after dinner, at the mess of the Flying School on Salisbury Plain, he started a debate as to what will be the most permanent danger which airmen will have to encounter. Having listened to successive opinions as to air-pockets, faulty construction, and over-banking, he ended by shrugging his shoulders and refusing to put forward his own views, though he gave the impression that they differed from any advanced by his companions.

It is worth remarking that after his own complete disappearance it was found that his private affairs were arranged with a precision which may show that he had a strong premonition of disaster. With these essential explanations I will now give the narrative exactly as it stands, beginning at page three of the blood-soaked note-book:

"Nevertheless, when I dined at Rheims with Coselli and Gustav Raymond I found that neither of them was aware of any particular danger in the higher layers of the atmosphere. I did not actually say what was in my thoughts, but I got so near to it that if they had any corresponding idea they could not have failed to express it. But then they are two empty, vainglorious fellows with no thought beyond seeing their silly names in the newspaper. It is interesting to note that neither of them had ever been much beyond the twenty-thousand-foot level. Of course, men have been higher than this both in balloons and in the ascent of mountains. It must be well above that point that the aeroplane enters the danger zone—always presuming that my premonitions are correct.

"Aeroplaning has been with us now for more than twenty years, and one might well ask: Why should this peril be only revealing itself in our day? The answer is obvious. In the old days of weak engines, when a hundred horse-power Gnome or Green was considered ample for every need, the flights were very restricted. Now that three hundred horse-power is the rule rather than the exception, visits to the upper layers have become easier and more common. Some of us can remember how, in our youth, Garros made a world-wide reputation by attaining nineteen thousand feet, and it was considered a remarkable achievement to fly over the Alps. Our standard now has been immeasurably raised, and there are twenty high flights for one in former years. Many of them have been undertaken with impunity. The thirty-thousand-foot level has been reached time after time with no dis-comfort beyond cold and asthma. What does this prove? A visitor might descend upon this planet a thousand times and never see a tiger. Yet tigers exist, and if he chanced to come down into a jungle he might be devoured. There are jungles of the upper air, and there are worse things than tigers which inhabit them. I believe in time they will map these jungles accurately out. Even at the present moment I could name two of them. One of them lies over the Pau-Biarritz district of France. Another is just over my head as I write here in my house in Wiltshire. I rather think there is a third in the Homburg-Wiesbaden district.

"It was the disappearance of the airmen that first set me thinking. Of course, everyone said that they had fallen into the sea, but that did not satisfy me at all. First, there was Verrier in France; his machine was found near Bayonne, but they never got his body. There was the case of Baxter also, who vanished, though his engine and some of the iron fixings were found in a wood in Leicestershire. In that case, Dr. Middleton, of Amesbury, who was watching the flight with a telescope, declares that just before the clouds obscured the view he saw the machine, which was at an enormous height, suddenly rise perpendicularly upwards in a succession of jerks in a manner that he would have thought to be im-possible. That was the last seen of Baxter. There was a correspondence in the papers, but it never led to anything. There were several other similar cases, and then there was the death of Hay Connor. What a cackle there was about an unsolved mystery of the air, and what columns in the halfpenny papers, and yet how little was ever done to get to the bottom of the business! He came down in a tremendous vol-plane from an unknown height. He never got off his machine and died in his pilot's seat. Died of what? 'Heart disease,' said the doctors. Rubbish! Hay Connor's heart was as sound as mine is. What did Venables say? Venables was the only man who was at his side when he died. He said that he was shivering and looked like a man who had been badly scared. 'Died of fright,' said Venables, but could not imagine what he was frightened about. Only said one word to Venables, which sounded like 'Monstrous.' They could make nothing of that at the inquest. But I could make something of it. Monsters! That was the last word of poor Harry Hay Connor. And he DID die of fright, just as Venables thought.

"And then there was Myrtle's head. Do you really believe—does anybody really believe—that a man's head could be driven clean into his body by the force of a fall? Well, perhaps it may be possible, but I, for one, have never believed that it was so with Myrtle. And the grease upon his clothes—'all slimy with grease,' said somebody at the inquest. Queer that nobody got thinking after that! I did—but, then, I had been thinking for a good long time. I've made three ascents—how Dangerfield used to chaff me about my shot-gun—but I've never been high enough. Now, with this new, light Paul Veroner machine and its one hundred and seventy-five Robur, I should easily touch the thirty thousand tomorrow. I'll have a shot at the record. Maybe I shall have a shot at something else as well. Of course, it's dangerous. If a fellow wants to avoid danger he had best keep out of flying altogether and subside finally into flannel slippers and a dressing-gown. But I'll visit the air-jungle tomorrow—and if there's anything there I shall know it. If I return, I'll find myself a bit of a celebrity. If I don't this note-book may explain what I am trying to do, and how I lost my life in doing it. But no drivel about accidents or mysteries, if YOU please.

"I chose my Paul Veroner monoplane for the job. There's nothing like a monoplane when real work is to be done. Beaumont found that out in very early days. For one thing it doesn't mind damp, and the weather looks as if we should be in the clouds all the time. It's a bonny little model and answers my hand like a tender-mouthed horse. The engine is a ten-cylinder rotary Robur working up to one hundred and seventy-five. It has all the modern improvements—enclosed fuselage, high-curved landing skids, brakes, gyroscopic steadiers, and three speeds, worked by an alteration of the angle of the planes upon the Venetian-blind principle. I took a shot-gun with me and a dozen cartridges filled with buck-shot. You should have seen the face of Perkins, my old mechanic, when I directed him to put them in. I was dressed like an Arctic explorer, with two jerseys under my overalls, thick socks inside my padded boots, a storm-cap with flaps, and my talc goggles. It was stifling outside the hangars, but I was going for the summit of the Himalayas, and had to dress for the part. Perkins knew there was something on and implored me to take him with me. Perhaps I should if I were using the biplane, but a monoplane is a one-man show—if you want to get the last foot of life out of it. Of course, I took an oxygen bag; the man who goes for the altitude record without one will either be frozen or smothered—or both.

"I had a good look at the planes, the rudder-bar, and the elevating lever before I got in. Everything was in order so far as I could see. Then I switched on my engine and found that she was running sweetly. When they let her go she rose almost at once upon the lowest speed. I circled my home field once or twice just to warm her up, and then with a wave to Perkins and the others, I flattened out my planes and put her on her highest. She skimmed like a swallow down wind for eight or ten miles until I turned her nose up a little and she began to climb in a great spiral for the cloud-bank above me. It's all-important to rise slowly and adapt yourself to the pressure as you go.

"It was a close, warm day for an English September, and there was the hush and heaviness of impending rain. Now and then there came sudden puffs of wind from the south-west—one of them so gusty and unexpected that it caught me napping and turned me half-round for an instant. I remember the time when gusts and whirls and air-pockets used to be things of danger—before we learned to put an overmastering power into our engines. Just as I reached the cloud-banks, with the altimeter marking three thousand, down came the rain. My word, how it poured! It drummed upon my wings and lashed against my face, blurring my glasses so that I could hardly see. I got down on to a low speed, for it was painful to travel against it. As I got higher it became hail, and I had to turn tail to it. One of my cylinders was out of action—a dirty plug, I should imagine, but still I was rising steadily with plenty of power. After a bit the trouble passed, whatever it was, and I heard the full, deep-throated purr—the ten singing as one.

That's where the beauty of our modern silencers comes in. We can at last control our engines by ear. How they squeal and squeak and sob when they are in trouble! All those cries for help were wasted in the old days, when every sound was swallowed up by the monstrous racket of the machine. If only the early aviators could come back to see the beauty and perfection of the mechanism which have been bought at the cost of their lives!

"About nine-thirty I was nearing the clouds. Down below me, all blurred and shadowed with rain, lay the vast expanse of Salisbury Plain. Half a dozen flying machines were doing hackwork at the thousand-foot level, looking like little black swallows against the green background. I dare say they were wondering what I was doing up in cloud-land. Suddenly a grey curtain drew across beneath me and the wet folds of vapours were swirling round my face. It was clammily cold and miserable. But I was above the hail-storm, and that was something gained. The cloud was as dark and thick as a London fog. In my anxiety to get clear, I cocked her nose up until the automatic alarm-bell rang, and I actually began to slide backwards. My sopped and dripping wings had made me heavier than I thought, but presently I was in lighter cloud, and soon had cleared the first layer. There was a second—opal-coloured and fleecy—at a great height above my head, a white, unbroken ceiling above, and a dark, unbroken floor below, with the monoplane labouring upwards upon a vast spiral between them. It is deadly lonely in these cloud-spaces. Once a great flight of some small water-birds went past me, flying very fast to the westwards. The quick whir of their wings and their musical cry were cheery to my ear. I fancy that they were teal, but I am a wretched zoologist. Now that we humans have become birds we must really learn to know our brethren by sight.

"The wind down beneath me whirled and swayed the broad cloud-plain. Once a great eddy formed in it, a whirlpool of vapour, and through it, as down a funnel, I caught sight of the distant world. A large white biplane was passing at a vast depth beneath me. I fancy it was the morning mail service betwixt Bristol and London. Then the drift swirled inwards again and the great solitude was unbroken.

"Just after ten I touched the lower edge of the upper cloud-stratum. It consisted of fine, diaphanous vapour drifting swiftly from the westwards. The wind had been steadily rising all this time and it was now blowing a sharp breeze—twenty-eight an hour by my gauge. Already it was very cold, though my altimeter only marked nine thousand. The engines were working beautifully, and we went droning steadily upwards. The cloud-bank was thicker than I had expected, but at last it thinned out into a golden mist before me, and then in an instant I had shot out from it, and there was an unclouded sky and a brilliant sun above my head—all blue and gold above, all shining silver below, one vast, glimmering plain as far as my eyes could reach. It was a quarter past ten o'clock, and the barograph needle pointed to twelve thousand eight hundred. Up I went and up, my ears concentrated upon the deep purring of my motor, my eyes busy always with the watch, the revolution indicator, the petrol lever, and the oil pump. No wonder aviators are said to be a fearless race. With so many things to think of there is no time to trouble about oneself. It was about this time I noted how unreliable is the compass when above a certain height from earth. At fifteen thousand feet mine was pointing east and a point south. The sun and the wind gave me my true bearings.

"I had hoped to reach an eternal stillness in these high altitudes, but with every thousand feet of ascent the gale grew stronger. My machine groaned and trembled in every joint and rivet as she faced it, and swept away like a sheet of paper when I banked her on the turn, skimming down wind at a greater pace, perhaps, than ever mortal man has moved. Yet I had always to turn again and tack up in the wind's eye, for it was not merely a height record that I was after. By all my calculations it was above little Wiltshire that my air-jungle lay, and all my labour might be lost if I struck the outer layers at some farther point.

"When I reached the nineteen-thousand-foot level, which was about midday, the wind was so severe that I looked with some anxiety to the stays of my wings, expecting momentarily to see them snap or slacken. I even cast loose the parachute behind me, and fastened its hook into the ring of my leathern belt, so as to be ready for the worst. Now was the time when a bit of scamped work by the mechanic is paid for by the life of the aeronaut. But she held together bravely. Every cord and strut was humming and vibrating like so many harp-strings, but it was glorious to see how, for all the beating and the buffeting, she was still the conqueror of

Nature and the mistress of the sky. There is surely something divine in man himself that he should rise so superior to the limitations which Creation seemed to impose—rise, too, by such unselfish, heroic devotion as this air-conquest has shown. Talk of human degeneration! When has such a story as this been written in the annals of our race?

"These were the thoughts in my head as I climbed that monstrous, inclined plane with the wind sometimes beating in my face and sometimes whistling behind my ears, while the cloud-land beneath me fell away to such a distance that the folds and hummocks of silver had all smoothed out into one flat, shining plain. But suddenly I had a horrible and unprecedented experience. I have known before what it is to be in what our neighbours have called a tourbillon, but never on such a scale as this. That huge, sweeping river of wind of which I have spoken had, as it appears, whirlpools within it which were as monstrous as itself. Without a moment's warning I was dragged suddenly into the heart of one. I spun round for a minute or two with such velocity that I almost lost my senses, and then fell suddenly, left wing foremost, down the vacuum funnel in the centre. I dropped like a stone, and lost nearly a thousand feet. It was only my belt that kept me in my seat, and the shock and breathlessness left me hanging half-insensible over the side of the fuselage. But I am always capable of a supreme effort—it is my one great merit as an aviator. I was conscious that the descent was slower. The whirlpool was a cone rather than a funnel, and I had come to the apex. Then, with a terrific wrench, throwing my weight all to one side, I levelled my planes and brought her head away from the wind. In an instant I had shot out of the eddies and was skimming down the sky. Then, shaken but victorious, I turned her nose up and began once more my steady grind on the upward spiral. I took a large sweep to avoid the danger-spot of the whirlpool, and soon I was safely above it. Just after one o'clock I was twenty-one thousand feet above the sea-level. To my great joy I had topped the gale, and with every hundred feet of ascent the air grew stiller. On the other hand, it was very cold, and I was conscious of that peculiar nausea which goes with rarefaction of the air. For the first time I unscrewed the mouth of my oxygen bag and took an occasional whiff of the glorious gas. I could feel it running like a cordial through my veins, and I was exhilarated almost to the point of drunkenness. I shouted and sang as I soared upwards into the cold, still outer world.

"It is very clear to me that the insensibility which came upon Glaisher, and in a lesser degree upon Coxwell, when, in 1862, they ascended in a balloon to the height of thirty thousand feet, was due to the extreme speed with which a perpendicular ascent is made. Doing it at an easy gradient and accustoming oneself to the lessened barometric pressure by slow degrees, there are no such dreadful symptoms. At the same great height I found that even without my oxygen inhaler I could breathe without undue distress. It was bitterly cold, however, and my thermometer was at zero Fahrenheit. At one-thirty I was nearly seven miles above the surface of the earth, and still ascending steadily. I found, however, that the rarefied air was giving markedly less support to my planes, and that my angle of ascent had to be considerably lowered in consequence. It was already clear that even with my light weight and strong engine-power there was a point in front of me where I should be held. To make matters worse, one of my sparking-plugs was in trouble again and there was intermittent misfiring in the engine. My heart was heavy with the fear of failure.

"It was about that time that I had a most extraordinary experience. Something whizzed past me in a trail of smoke and exploded with a loud, hissing sound, sending forth a cloud of steam. For the instant I could not imagine what had happened. Then I remembered that the earth is for ever being bombarded by meteor stones, and would be hardly inhabitable were they not in nearly every case turned to vapour in the outer layers of the atmosphere. Here is a new danger for the high-altitude man, for two others passed me when I was nearing the forty-thousand-foot mark. I cannot doubt that at the edge of the earth's envelope the risk would be a very real one.

"My barograph needle marked forty-one thousand three hundred when I became aware that I could go no farther. Physically, the strain was not as yet greater than I could bear but my machine had reached its limit. The attenuated air gave no firm support to the wings, and the least tilt developed into side-slip, while she seemed sluggish on her controls. Possibly, had the engine been at its best, another thousand feet might have been within our capacity, but it was still misfiring, and two out of the ten cylinders appeared to be out of action. If I had not already reached the zone for which I was searching then I should never see it upon this journey. But was it not possible that I had attained it? Soaring in circles like a monstrous hawk upon the forty-thousand-foot level I let the monoplane guide herself, and with my Mannheim glass I made a careful observation of my surroundings. The heavens were perfectly clear; there was no indication of those dangers which I had imagined.

"I have said that I was soaring in circles. It struck me suddenly that I would do well to take a wider sweep and open up a new airtract. If the hunter entered an earth-jungle he would drive through it if he wished to find his game. My reasoning had led me to believe that the air-jungle which I had imagined lay somewhere over Wiltshire. This should be to the south and west of me. I took my bearings from the sun, for the compass was hopeless and no trace of earth was to be seen—nothing but the distant, silver cloud-plain. However, I got my direction as best I might and kept her head straight to the mark. I reckoned that my petrol supply would not last for more than another hour or so, but I could afford to use it to the last drop, since a single magnificent vol-plane could at any time take me to the earth.

"Suddenly I was aware of something new. The air in front of me had lost its crystal clearness. It was full of long, ragged wisps of something which I can only compare to very fine cigarette smoke. It hung about in wreaths and coils, turning and twisting slowly in the sunlight. As the monoplane shot through it, I was aware of a faint taste of oil upon my lips, and there was a greasy scum upon the woodwork of the machine. Some infinitely fine organic matter appeared to be suspended in the atmosphere. There was no life there. It was inchoate and diffuse, extending for many square acres and then fringing off into the void. No, it was not life. But might it not be the remains of life? Above all, might it not be the food of life, of monstrous life, even as the humble grease of the ocean is the food for the mighty whale? The thought was in my mind when my eyes looked upwards and I saw the most wonderful vision that ever man has seen. Can I hope to convey it to you even as I saw it myself last Thursday?

"Conceive a jelly-fish such as sails in our summer seas, bell-shaped and of enormous size—far larger, I should judge, than the dome of St. Paul's. It was of a light pink colour veined with a delicate green, but the whole huge fabric so tenuous that it was but a fairy outline against the dark blue sky. It pulsated with a delicate and regular rhythm. From it there depended two long, drooping, green tentacles, which swayed slowly backwards and forwards. This gorgeous vision passed gently with noiseless dignity over my head, as light and fragile as a soap-bubble, and drifted upon its stately way.

"I had half-turned my monoplane, that I might look after this beautiful creature, when, in a moment, I found myself amidst a perfect fleet of them, of all sizes, but none so large as the first. Some were quite small, but the majority about as big as an average balloon, and with much the same curvature at the top. There was in them a delicacy of texture and colouring which reminded me of the finest Venetian glass. Pale shades of pink and green were the prevailing tints, but all had a lovely iridescence where the sun shimmered through their dainty forms. Some hundreds of them drifted past me, a wonderful fairy squadron of strange unknown argosies of the sky—creatures whose forms and substance were so attuned to these pure heights that one could not conceive anything so delicate within actual sight or sound of earth.

"But soon my attention was drawn to a new phenomenon— the serpents of the outer air. These were long, thin, fantastic coils of vapour-like material, which turned and twisted with great speed, flying round and round at such a pace that the eyes could hardly follow them. Some of these ghost-like creatures were twenty or thirty feet long, but it was difficult to tell their girth, for their outline was so hazy that it seemed to fade away into the air around them. These air-snakes were of a very light grey or smoke colour, with some darker lines within, which gave the impression of a definite organism. One of them whisked past my very face, and I was conscious of a cold, clammy contact, but their composition was so unsubstantial that I could not connect them with any thought of physical danger, any more than the beautiful bell-like creatures which had preceded them. There was no more solidity in their frames than in the floating spume from a broken wave.

"But a more terrible experience was in store for me. Floating downwards from a great height there came a purplish patch of vapour, small as I saw it first, but rapidly enlarging as it approached me, until it appeared to be hundreds of square feet in size. Though fashioned of some transparent, jelly-like substance, it was none the less of much more definite outline and solid consistence than anything which I had seen before. There were more traces, too, of a physical organization, especially two vast, shadowy, circular plates upon either side, which may have been eyes, and a perfectly solid white projection between them which was as curved and cruel as the beak of a vulture.

"The whole aspect of this monster was formidable and threatening, and it kept changing its colour from a very light mauve to a dark, angry purple so thick that it cast a shadow as it drifted between my monoplane and the sun. On the upper curve of its huge body there were three great projections which I can only describe as enormous bubbles, and I was convinced as I looked at them that they were charged with some extremely light gas which served to buoy up the misshapen and semi-solid mass in the rarefied air. The creature moved swiftly along, keeping pace easily with the monoplane, and for twenty miles or more it formed my horrible escort, hovering over me like a bird of prey which is waiting to pounce. Its method of progression—done so swiftly that it was not easy to follow—was to throw out a long, glutinous streamer in front of it, which in turn seemed to draw forward the rest of the writhing body. So elastic and gelatinous was it that never for two successive minutes was it the same shape, and yet each change made it more threatening and loathsome than the last.

"I knew that it meant mischief. Every purple flush of its hideous body told me so. The vague, goggling eyes which were turned always upon me were cold and merciless in their viscid hatred. I dipped the nose of my monoplane downwards to escape it. As I did so, as quick as a flash there shot out a long tentacle from this mass of floating blubber, and it fell as light and sinuous as a whip-lash across the front of my machine. There was a loud hiss as it lay for a moment across the hot engine, and it whisked itself into the air again, while the huge, flat body drew itself together as if in sudden pain. I dipped to a vol-pique, but again a tentacle fell over the monoplane and was shorn off by the propeller as easily as it might have cut through a smoke wreath. A long, gliding, sticky, serpent-like coil came from behind and caught me round the waist, dragging me out of the fuselage. I tore at it, my fingers sinking into the smooth, glue-like surface, and for an instant I disengaged myself, but only to be caught round the boot by another coil, which gave me a jerk that tilted me almost on to my back.

"As I fell over I blazed off both barrels of my gun, though, indeed, it was like attacking an elephant with a pea-shooter to imagine that any human weapon could cripple that mighty bulk. And yet I aimed better than I knew, for, with a loud report, one of the great blisters upon the creature's back exploded with the puncture of the buck-shot. It was very clear that my conjecture was right, and that these vast, clear bladders were distended with some lifting gas, for in an instant the huge, cloud-like body turned sideways, writhing desperately to find its balance, while the white beak snapped and gaped in horrible fury. But already I had shot away on the steepest glide that I dared to attempt, my engine still full on, the flying propeller and the force of gravity shooting me downwards like an aerolite. Far behind me I saw a dull, purplish smudge growing swiftly smaller and merging into the blue sky behind it. I was safe out of the deadly jungle of the outer air.

"Once out of danger I throttled my engine, for nothing tears a machine to pieces quicker than running on full power from a height. It was a glorious, spiral vol-plane from nearly eight miles of altitude—first, to the level of the silver cloud-bank, then to that of the storm-cloud beneath it, and finally, in beating rain, to the surface of the earth. I saw the Bristol Channel beneath me as I broke from the clouds, but, having still some petrol in my tank, I got twenty miles inland before I found myself stranded in a field half a mile from the village of Ashcombe. There I got three tins of petrol from a passing motor-car, and at ten minutes past six that evening I alighted gently in my own home meadow at Devizes, after such a journey as no mortal upon earth has ever yet taken and lived to tell the tale. I have seen the beauty and I have seen the horror of the heights—and greater beauty or greater horror than that is not within the ken of man.

"And now it is my plan to go once again before I give my results to the world. My reason for this is that I must surely have something to show by way of proof before I lay such a tale before my fellow-men. It is true that others will soon follow and will confirm what I have said, and yet I should wish to carry conviction from the first. Those lovely iridescent bubbles of the air should not be hard to capture. They drift slowly upon their way, and the swift monoplane could intercept their leisurely course. It is likely enough that they would dissolve in the heavier layers of the atmosphere, and that some small heap of amorphous jelly might be all that I should bring to earth with me. And yet something there would surely be by which I could substantiate my story. Yes, I will go, even if I run a risk by doing so. These purple horrors would not seem to be numerous. It is probable that I shall not see one. If I do I shall dive at once. At the worst there is always the shot-gun and my knowledge of…"

Here a page of the manuscript is unfortunately missing. On the next page is written, in large, straggling writing:

"Forty-three thousand feet. I shall never see earth again. They are beneath me, three of them. God help me; it is a dreadful death to die!"

Such in its entirety is the Joyce-Armstrong Statement. Of the man nothing has since been seen. Pieces of his shattered monoplane have been picked up inside the preserves of Mr. Budd-Lushington upon the borders of Kent and Sussex, within a few miles of the spot where the note-book was discovered. If the unfortunate aviator's theory is correct that this air-jungle, as he called it, existed only over the south-west of England, then it would seem that he had fled from it at the full speed of his monoplane, but had been overtaken and devoured by these horrible creatures at some spot in the outer atmosphere above the place where the grim relics were found. The picture of that monoplane skimming down the sky, with the nameless terrors flying as swiftly beneath it and cutting it off always from the earth while they gradually closed in upon their victim, is one upon which a man who valued his sanity would prefer not to dwell. There are many, as I am aware, who still jeer at the facts which I have here set down, but even they must admit that Joyce-Armstrong has disappeared, and I would commend to them his own words:

"This note-book may explain what I am trying to do, and how I lost my life in doing it. But no drivel about accidents or mysteries, if YOU please."

About the Authors

STEVE BILLINGS lives and works on the edge of The Cotswolds, near the city of Bath in the United Kingdom. Despite a life-long addiction to bleak music and dark literature, he lives a chaotic but happy life with his wife, two children, and a pair of deranged cats. His first ever short story finished as runner-up in the 2012 Aeon Award competition and was published in Albedo One magazine. He has huge respect for independent publishers and is delighted to be part of this anthology.

FRANK COLLIA hails from Parts Unknown (well, the greater P.U. metroplex) and now lives in Tampa, Florida where he writes author bios in the third person and stays mostly inside during the summer. His short fiction has been featured in *Dead Worlds 4*, *Bigfoot Terror Tales Vol. 1*, and *Boroughs of the Dead 2*.

CATHERINE EDMUNDS began her professional life as a musician, having trained at Dartington College of Arts and the National Centre for Orchestral Studies, Goldsmith's College, London. Two decades later, she changed direction and reinvented herself as a writer and artist. She still teaches music from her home in North East England, but spends more time as an author and illustrator. Works for Circaidy Gregory Press include her poetry collection *wormwood, earth and honey*; the magical realism novel *Small Poisons*—a contemporary tale for Midsummer Night's dreamers; and *Serpentine*, exploring what happens when art doesn't only reflect life but is life itself. Her latest novel is *Bacchus Wynd*, an intense tale of personal re-invention. Competition successes for poetry include two shortlistings for the Bridport Prize and a Pushcart Prize nomination; and for fiction, runner-up in the Roy Wood Memorial competition, placed in the Sid Chaplin competition, several shortlistings in Flash 500, and many others. Catherine has regularly exhibited paintings in County Durham, and in 2013 appeared on television in the Glasgow heats of *Sky Portrait Artist of the Year*. She is currently working on a biography of her Holocaust-survivor mother.

KC GRIFANT is an award-winning science writer specializing in technology, biology, and astronomy. She has written cover features for national publications on prototype robots that walk, talk and learn; wearable electronics; sunspot cycles; and metabolic "switches" for cancer. She has met several living writing inspirations: Margaret Atwood, Joe Haldeman, R.L. Stine, and William Gibson. Her creative endeavors are fueled by Taco Tuesdays, indie comics, and 100% Kona coffee.

DANIEL HALE is an up-and-coming storyteller living in Ohio, USA. He has been published in *Revolt Daily*, the *All Hallow's Evil* anthology of Mystery and Horror, LLC, and *The Last Diner* anthology of Knightwatch Press. When not writing he spends his days buying books faster than he can read them and worshiping all things British.

ASHLEY NORRIS HURD is currently querying her debut novel, a young adult fantasy entitled *Gemin*. She is co-organizer of the Central PA Writers Workshop, an amazing group of encouraging and supportive writers. When she's not writing, she's usually teaching her crazy, fun alternative education students or taking road trips with her wonderful husband, Chuck, to see family, friends, or NASCAR races.

THOMAS KLEATON is a freelance horror writer. He has had stories published online in SNM Horror Magazine and on the Hellnotes and Necon eBooks websites. His stories have appeared in the horror anthologies *Cellar Door: Words of Beauty*, *Tales of Terror*, *Serial Killers Tres Trias*, and *Bones*.

LISAMARIE LAMB started writing in her late teens, but it was only with the birth of her daughter that she decided to write more seriously, with the aim of publication. Since that decision in 2010, she has had over 30 short stories published in anthologies and magazines. In November 2012, Dark Hall Press published a collection of her short stories with a twist, entitled *Over The Bridge*. In November 2013, J. Ellington Ashton Press released a second short story collection entitled *Fairy Lights*. She has also collaborated on a project entitled *A Roof Over Their Heads*, written by six authors from the Isle of Sheppey, about the island where she lives with her husband, daughter, and two cats.

VINCE LIBERATO is a longtime enthusiast of Bikram yoga, member of an iron-willed yet loving family, property of his girlfriend Micole, and owner of a dog named Pony. He has been featured twice in genre anthologies published by Third Flatiron Press (*Intelligence* and *Redshifted: Martian Stories*), every volume of the *Demonic Visions* series, as well as Almond Press's *After the Fall, Tales of the Apocalypse* and Horrified Press's *Tales of the Undead: Undead in Pictures*. He lives in Texas.

JAMES AUSTIN McCORMICK is a college lecturer from England who enjoys all types of speculative fiction—science fiction, horror, and fantasy especially—and often tries to blend these elements together in his own writing. He is also a particular fan of classic Gothic and Victorian horror tales. James has had many works published professionally, most recently two science fiction novels, *Dragon* and *Sunfall*, both published by Class Act Books. In addition, he has also had several novellas and short stories published in various publications. These include a vampire western "Sundown" in the horror anthology *Deathgrip*, a fantasy comedy "Tommy and the Trolls" in the anthology *Strangely Funny*, and dozens of shorts in such magazines as Jupiter SF, Tales of the Talisman, and Thirteen Stories. Continuum SF also published a series of his science fiction tales from 2004 until 2006. James has two more novels out in the next year: *Balec*, a supernatural horror, and *The Last Synn*, a sword and sorcery fantasy inspired by his two writing heroes H.P. Lovecraft and Robert E. Howard.

BEN PIENAAR presently clings to dear life in Melbourne, Australia. To support his debilitating coffee and writing habits he works two jobs, one teaching children English and another selling alcohol to the masses. He has three to five vivid nightmares per week, often using these as inspiration for his stories. He has recently attained a Bachelor of Arts at Deakin University but still refuses to get a real job, preferring instead to hide in his dark, rat-ridden house and read copious books. He has had eleven short stories published to date in various magazines and anthologies, and is currently working on a novel about a mythological beast no one seems to have heard of.

EVAN PURCELL is an American working and living in rural China, a land of ancient traditions, friendly people, and absolutely no cheese within a hundred mile radius. Except for that last part, he loves living there. By day, he teaches high school English and volunteers in the surrounding villages. By night, he sings bad karaoke. He also writes a lot of stories—a slightly nobler pastime than singing "Sweet Caroline" with a bunch of inebriated Chinese people—which have appeared in Cracked.com, Niteblade Magazine, and Prizm Books. Despite all that, he's a normal guy, not nearly as weird as his short stories would imply. In fact, if you see him walking down the street, feel free to stop and say hello. And if you offer him some nice American cheese, he will be forever in your debt.

LIZZ-AYN SHAARAWI is a Texan lost in the Oregonian wilderness. She is a horror screenwriter and author whose short stories have been featured in numerous anthologies, including *In the Bloodstream*, *Ain't No Sanity Claus*, and *Fortunes: Lost and Found*. Her screenplays were recognized by the Austin Film Festival, the Nicholl Fellowship in Screenwriting, and the Page Awards. She enjoys cheap thrills, expensive shoes, and things that go bump in the night.

PAUL STARKEY lives in Nottingham, England, but would like to make it clear that he has no information pertaining to the whereabouts of Robin Hood, and is assuredly NOT a Merry Man. He has been writing for many years and has been published on both sides of the Atlantic, most notably by the British Fantasy Society. He's written four novels, the first of which, *City of Caves*, he self-published, and is currently at work on his fifth. He's also published an ebook of short stories, *The Devils of Amber Street*. He regularly blogs about writing and reviews films. His preferred genres are science fiction, horror, fantasy, and crime, and he especially likes to mix genres. Occasionally some romance may sneak into his work, but he's yet to write anything where something odd didn't happen or someone wasn't horribly killed.

Please check out the authors' websites, follow them on Twitter, 'Like' their Facebook pages, and become a fan of them on Goodreads. They value your support.

About the Editor

Sawney Hatton is an author, editor, and screenwriter. His debut Dark Comedy novel **Dead Size**, his dark Young Adult novel **Uglyville**, and his dark Short Story collection **Everyone Is a Moon** were released by Dark Park Publishing.

Other incarnations of Sawney have produced marketing videos, attended Scottish Highland games, and played the banjo and sousaphone (not at the same time). As of this writing he is still very much alive.

Visit the author's website at
www.SawneyHatton.com

Acknowledgments

All of us here at Dark Park Publishing would like to thank the following folks for their sundry support:

Lauren Eveland
William & Catherine Philbrick
Willi Schulz
Martha Macartney
Meme Eveland & Paul Griffin
Ed Eveland
Stephanie Reyer & Thomas Romer
Christopher Scanlon
Jim Woods
Jason Myers
Julie Thielen
Lauren Banfitch
John McGinley
Dan Calvisi
Eirik Gumeny
Autumn M. Birt
Willow Ward
Laura Beth Roark-Harris
Mark Lee
The NoteBook Blogairy
Pubslush.com

Printed in Great Britain
by Amazon

20142034R00163